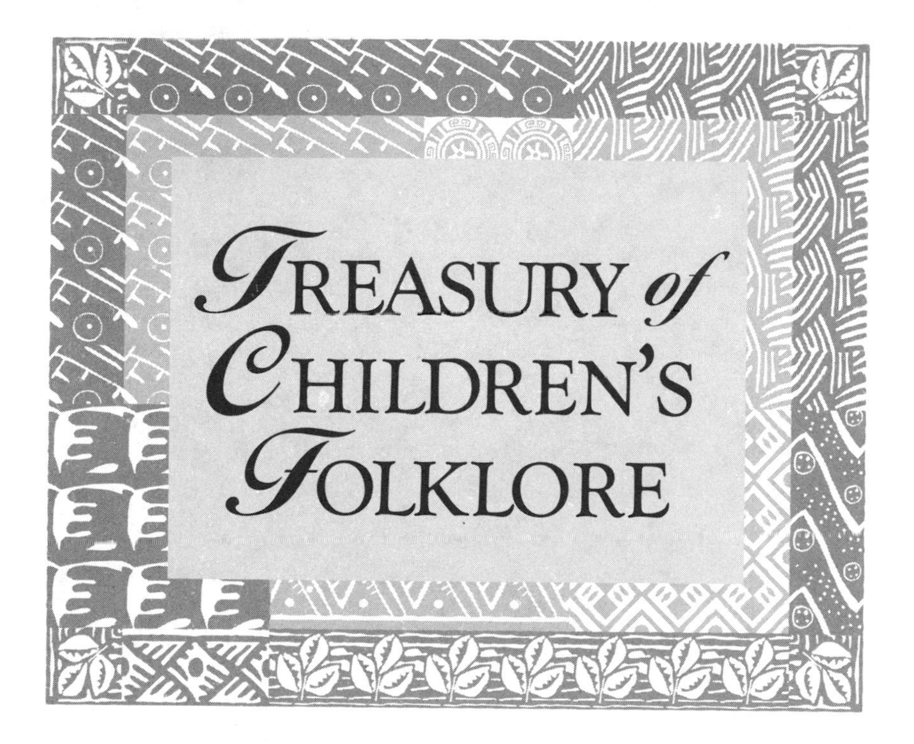
TREASURY of
CHILDREN'S
FOLKLORE

D0395245

TREASURY of CHILDREN'S FOLKLORE

BRIAN SCOTT SOCKIN
AND EILEEN L. WONG

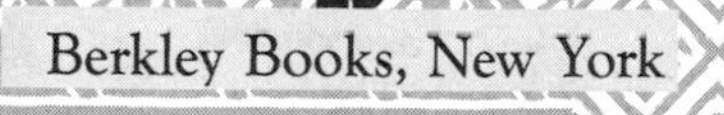
Berkley Books, New York

Kind permission was granted to reprint "The Royal Candlestick," retold by Hasan El-Shamy, Professor of Folklore at Indiana University, from his book *Folktales of Egypt*, The University of Chicago Press. "Boastfulness Versus True Generosity" by Blanche L. Serwer-Bernstein from *In the Tradition of Moses and Mohammed* is reprinted by kind permission of the publisher, Jason Aronson Inc., Northvale, NJ, © 1994.

CARE is a registered mark of the Cooperative for Assistance and Relief Everywhere, Inc. CARE, Inc. © 1995.
For additional information about CARE:
CARE, 151 Ellis Street, N.E., Atlanta, Georgia 30303-2426.
(800) 521-CARE.

TREASURY OF CHILDREN'S FOLKLORE

A Berkley Book / published by arrangement with the authors

PRINTING HISTORY
Berkley trade paperback edition / November 1995

For information address: The Berkley Publishing Group,
200 Madison Avenue, New York, New York 10016.

ISBN: 0-425-14977-3

BERKLEY®
Berkley Books are published by The Berkley Publishing Group,
200 Madison Avenue, New York, New York 10016.
BERKLEY and the "B" design
are trademarks belonging to Berkley Publishing Corporation.

PRINTED IN THE UNITED STATES OF AMERICA

10 9 8 7 6 5 4 3 2 1

ACKNOWLEDGMENTS

This book was made possible with the help and encouragement of many generous and caring individuals who freely gave their time and talents to "make a difference" for CARE.

We wish to thank everyone who researched and collected the folktales. Everyone we contacted has made their own significant contribution to this book.

A special thanks to all those who contributed folktales. We were overwhelmed by your generosity, and found it a very difficult task to make the final selection of stories to include in this book.

A very special thanks to Margaret Mills, professor of Folklore at the University of Pennsylvania, who was the catalyst in providing us with a folklore network of academics and storytellers. She was not only helpful but inspirational in helping us put this book together.

Also, a very special thanks to Professor Beverly Stoeltje of Indiana University, who opened the "folklore gateway" to both colleagues and graduate students who found the time to contribute stories or donate their expertise. Noted thanks to Professors John Johnson, Paul Newman, Roxanna Ma Newman, Frank Proschan, and

Hasan El-Shamy, and to folklore graduate students Rosemarie Kadende, Ramenga Osotsi, Emmanuel Ribeiro, and Sudha Rajagopolan.

We thank Barbara Baumgartner, a storyteller and children's author, who introduced us to many wonderful contributors from the Patchwork Guild of storytellers.

We thank our partners at CARE who called upon their worldwide network for folktale contributions. A noted thanks to LMichael Green and Anne Johnson who helped us shepherd this project to completion.

And finally, we thank our editor at Berkley, Elizabeth Beier, whose special and heartfelt attention helped to bring this book to its wonderful fruition.

Dear Reader:

For me, a good story is one that transports me to faraway places and introduces me to exciting new people and ideas. So you can imagine how much I enjoyed reading this book of folktales from the countries where CARE works to help the poor make better lives for themselves.

It is in celebration of CARE's 50th Anniversary that this book is published. The book in turn celebrates the diverse cultures that make up the world of CARE. They are cultures as rich and diverse as our own, many of them rooted in ancient traditions and ways of life that can be traced back thousands of years. It is from such civilizations that the stories you are about to read have emerged.

Many of these cultures, unfortunately, are under siege. Poverty in the developing world is sapping the vitality and productivity of entire societies. In Africa, one person in three is undernourished. More than eight million Africans are infected with the virus that causes AIDS, and entire communities have perished from the disease. Meanwhile, war and civil conflicts in scores of countries worldwide have driven more than forty million people from their homes and reduced them to wards of the international community.

These are just a few of the challenges we face around the world. They are challenges taken up every day by CARE personnel, some of whom submitted stories for inclusion in this book. We hope you'll keep these people, as well as the people they serve, in mind as you enjoy the folktales in this fascinating collection.

Sincerely,

Philip Johnston
CARE Foundation President

CONTENTS

AFRICAN STORIES

ASIAN STORIES

EUROPEAN STORIES

LATIN AMERICAN STORIES

MIDDLE EASTERN STORIES

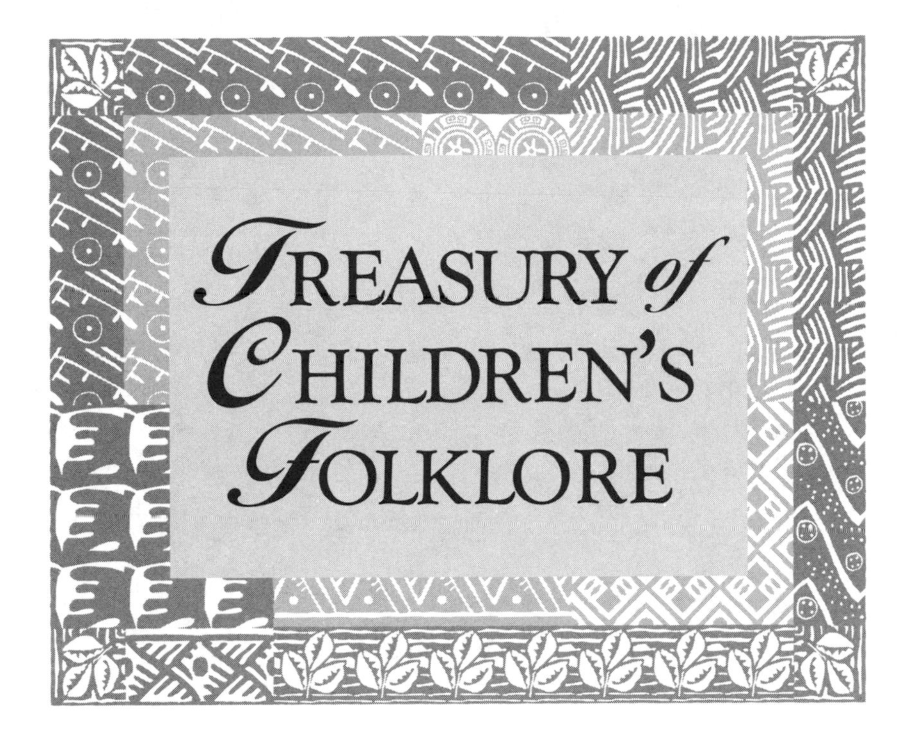
TREASURY of
CHILDREN'S
FOLKLORE

African Stories

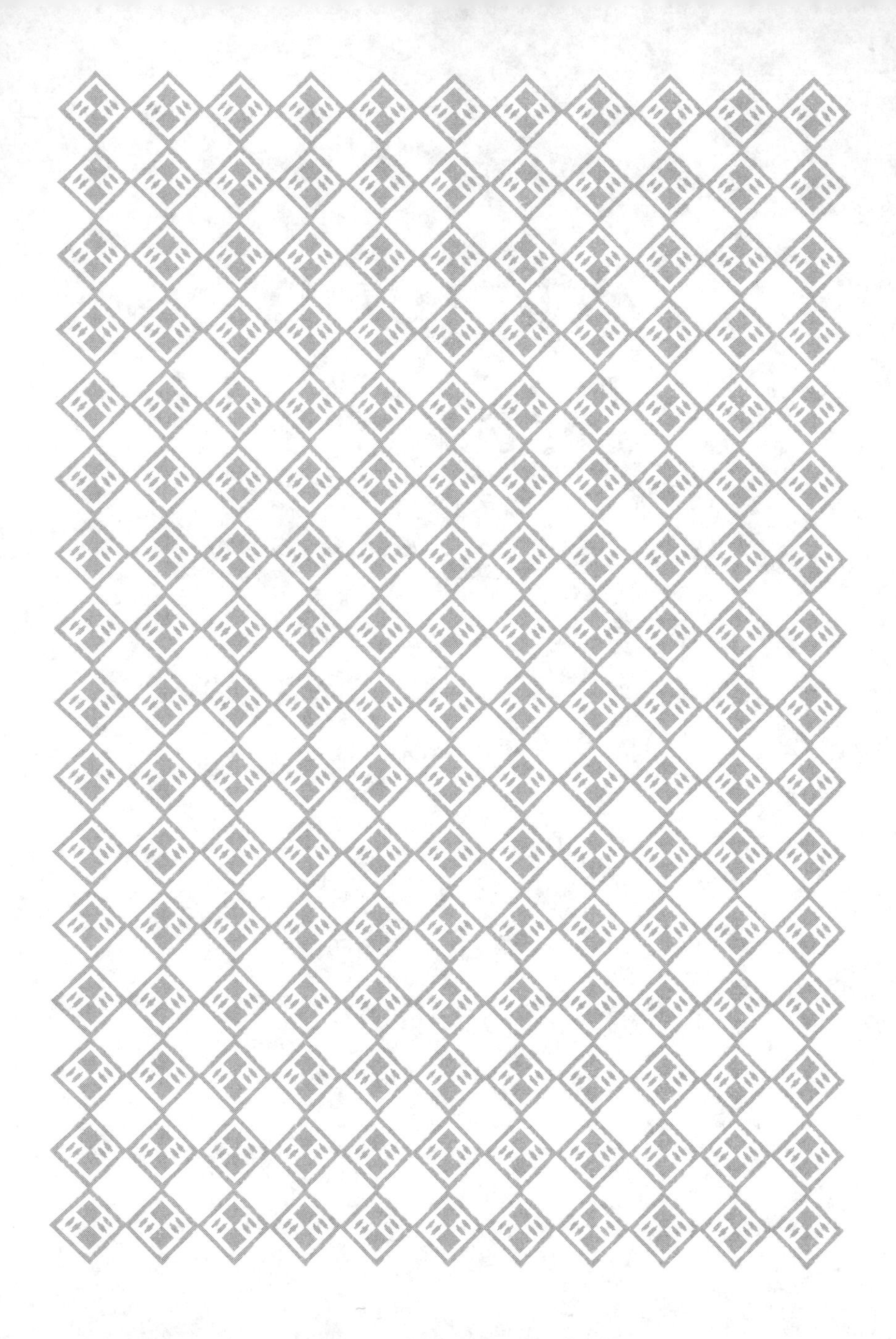

BURUNDI

The King and His Seven Wives

by Rosemarie Kadende

There once lived a king who had six beautiful wives. He showered his wives with his love and all of the material splendor that the kingdom had to offer.

All of the King's wives had children, but all were female. Alas, the King had only one wish—to have a male heir to his throne. Every year, the King's wives bore more children, but they always turned out to be little girls, not one was a boy.

One day the King decided to take a seventh wife in the hopes that she would give him a son. A year passed, and again, all of the wives, including the seventh, bore him more royal children. His first six wives, as expected, all had little girls, but the seventh produced a handsome baby boy who bore a mark in the form of the sun on his face.

The other six wives were so jealous of the seventh. She had only been the King's wife for a year but had quickly become his most favorite consort. The six jealous wives stole away with the boy infant and threw him into the river. An old woman found and rescued the baby before he could drown. She took the baby to her small home in the woods, and there she decided to raise him. Meanwhile, in the King's palace, the six scheming wives placed a snake in the baby boy's bed, and pretended that the seventh wife had borne a snake for a child. The King was outraged to learn of this mishap and scorned his seventh wife, threatening to divorce her. The seventh wife was bewildered and explained that she could not have been responsible for what had happened to her. Reluctantly, the King forgave her.

A year later all the wives again bore children. And again, all but the seventh wife had females. The seventh wife this time bore a beautiful son, who had the mark of the moon upon his face. And, as before, the six wives became enraged with jealousy and stole the baby from his bed and threw him into the same river. This time they replaced the boy with a puppy. The same old woman found the boy and took him into her care along with his older brother in her little domicile in the woods.

The King was now very angry indeed and feared the worst—that his seventh wife was cursed. The seventh wife, though, was brave and stout of heart, and with time, she again managed to convince the King that it was never her intention to have a puppy and she was therefore not responsible for its fate.

Once again, the King forgave her, warning her, however, that if they had another child that was not human, he would cast her out in a dark shadow of shame.

This time two years passed and the wives again had children. This time they were all female, including the seventh wife's baby. Her daughter bore the beautiful mark of a star on her face, which served to anger the six wives even more. Though not a boy, this daughter had something which theirs did not. Once more the six wives stole away with the child and cast her into the same river. And once again the same old woman found the baby girl and took her to her little home in the woods to care for her as she did her two brothers.

This time the King was filled with such rage that no one could appease him. And he did as he had promised, and had the seventh wife locked away in the dank, dark, and lonely dungeon beneath the palace, never to be seen again.

Every day the seventh wife gazed out of her small prison window. And though nobody outside could see who she was, they all assumed that she had committed a terrible crime since she was imprisoned in the deepest part of the dungeon. People who passed by and saw her cell window spit at her in shame. The King's guards gave her little to eat and little water to wash with, and her loveliness began to wilt into ugliness.

As the story goes, the old woman, meanwhile, raised the three children and they soon grew up to become very beautiful and happy young boys and girl. She taught them good manners and they enjoyed helping the old woman with the day's chores, as they believed that she was their mother.

One day the old woman, who had hidden away for days in the backroom of their little shabby home working on something secret, emerged from her studies. She called the children to gather around her and gave them a task—one more important than anything she had ever asked them to do! In the middle of the river, not far from their home, stood a strange and special tree that bore equally special leaves. She needed one of these wondrous leaves from the river, but she was too old to walk against the river's strong currents. So she asked the children for their help to obtain one of those precious leaves for her. She had warned them that there was danger involved in procuring one of these leaves, but the children agreed without question. They were only too happy to please and help the old woman who they thought to be their mother.

The oldest son went first, but before he left, he gave a stick to his brother and sister and told them that if something bad, very bad, were to happen to him, causing him to die, the stick would break in half and they would know of the fate that he had suffered.

The oldest son ventured forth, and on his way he met another old woman who asked where he was going in such a hurry. The oldest son had heard of this other old woman and that she was reputed to be wise in the ways of the woods and magic. But she was also known to be very nice to people that she liked and cruel to those she didn't. With the greatest respect he could muster, he greeted her and asked her how he might find and retrieve the special leaf in the river without harm. He told her of his quest for the leaf that grows on the tree in the middle of the river.

The old woman by the river showed him how to find the tree and where to enter the river. But she also warned him of the dangerous spell that surrounded the tree. She told him that should he hear voices calling his name while he was in the middle of the river, he must not turn around and look back, but should continue going straight until he reached the big tree, with its special leaves hanging from its branches. Once he plucked a leaf, only then could he turn for home and go back safely.

The oldest boy set out into the river and proceeded toward the tree, the river's powerful currents threatening to knock him off his feet and sweeping him downstream. Finally, as he approached the tree, he heard the voices calling him from behind. Though he tried to resist, the voices were so disturbing and alluring that he could not help himself, and he turned to look back. As he did this, just steps from the great tree, he suddenly turned into a stone.

Back at the old woman's home, the stick that he had given to his brother and sister broke in half and they learned of his fate.

The younger brother then took up the quest and, like his older brother, set out for the river. But before he left, he gave his sister a water pot and told her that should he die, the pot would break.

As he approached the river he met the same old woman with whom his brother had spoken. Having also heard odd tales of this strange old woman's wisdom and knowledge of magic, he asked her for her help in getting

the leaf from the tree in the river. She gave him the same instructions that she had given his brother. The second brother then set out into the river, fighting to keep his balance on the way.

When he was just steps from the big tree, he heard voices calling his name and, forgetting what he was told, turned around, suddenly turning into a stone.

At home, the water pot broke and his sister wept at discovering that her second brother had indeed perished in his quest. But she could not give up. Despite the danger, she put aside her fears and the anguish of the loss of her brothers. Mustering all the strength she could, she set out with keen resolve for the river to finish what had been started. She reached the river and, like her brothers, met the wise old woman, who reluctantly instructed her on how to retrieve the leaf from the big tree in the river. She tried to dissuade the girl from going into the river for fear that she would meet the same fate as her brothers. The sister, however, went on despite the old woman's warnings.

The girl waded into the river. Because she was so much lighter than her brothers, she had to fight against the strong currents even much more just to prevent herself from falling. But before she went very far, she remembered the old woman's warnings and, finding pieces of cotton in her dress, stuffed them in her ears.

As she approached the big tree in the river, the voices called out to her. She did not notice anything, as she could not hear the strange wails and cries. She reached the tree and plucked a single leaf from the tree. The leaf tingled in her hand and she touched her brothers with the very thing that they had given their lives to seek. Suddenly they both came back to life and they all hugged one another, so glad to be together again!

The three siblings made it back to shore safely with the leaf and gratefully thanked the wise old woman. When they arrived home, they proudly presented the leaf to the old woman who had raised them and recounted the story of their journey. She told them to touch the ground with the leaf, and when they did so, a beautiful house stood where their once shabby house had been. The house was indeed grand, filled with beautiful furniture and other nice things they never had dreamed of having. They shouted with delight and began their new life in comfort.

One day the King's guards were hunting in the woods where the three children lived and they saw this glorious house—which was even nicer than the King's palace! They saw the beautiful daughter tending the garden outside, beauty so wondrous to behold. They raced home to tell the King what they had seen, and the King sent his guards to bring the beautiful girl to his palace. When the

guards reached the house, however, the old woman who had cared for her and her brothers told the guards that the King must come himself.

The King returned later that very day, intrigued by his guards' stories. When he arrived, he was astonished at how much the children resembled him. The old woman told him the whole story of how she found them. Now, this was a pretty smart king, and he put two and two together, remembering what his seventh wife had told him. The age of the children matched exactly the age his seventh wife's children would have been. The King danced with glee—he had two sons all along and he did not know it. And his daughter—why, she was the most beautiful of all of his children.

He took the old woman and the three children back to the palace and presented them to his seventh wife, who had withered almost to nothing. The King released his seventh wife from prison and vowed to make up to her for all the terrible things that had happened to her. All she wanted was to be exonerated by the kingdom and to be with her children again. And so, this was the very first thing that the King did. He called for a celebration throughout the Kingdom and gathered all of the nobles and common folk together to make an announcement. He apologized to his seventh wife and cast his first six wives out of the palace, providing meager but ample housing in the woods for them to live out their rest of their lives in great shame. The King, his seventh wife—now his only wife—their three children, and the old woman all lived happily ever after.

BURUNDI:

Nestled in the heart of Central Africa, Burundi is a tiny, mountainous country with the second deepest lake in the world: Lake Tanganyika. Burundi is also one of Africa's poorest countries and in recent years many of its people have been displaced by political instability. CARE works to provide relief aid such as food, water and shelter to Burundians who have fled their homes.

The Hyena and the Lion

by Liben Jarson

Once upon a time, there lived a hyena. His wife had died, leaving nine very young sons behind. The hyena brought up his sons by hunting and scavenging for whatever food he could get. After a few years, realizing that his sons were strong and old enough to hunt for themselves, he called to them and said, "I am getting old. You are now all grown up. It is your turn to hunt. So, prove to me you can hunt—go and get us all some food."

All of them were delighted by their father's request. "Oh, Father, we thank you for giving us this honor. We have been looking forward to the fun of hunting." And with their father's blessing, the nine young hyenas went out to hunt.

As the hyenas were walking in the forest they met a lion. The lion asked them, "Where are you going?"

"We are out hunting for food," they replied.

"You know that I am the King of the Forest. I am braver and stronger than all other animals and you cannot go out hunting in the forest without my permission," said the lion.

"We know that and would like to seek your permission. Besides, we want to be your hunting partners," the hyenas said.

The lion agreed to take them as his partners and they joined together in a hunting party. On the second day they found nine bulls and an old cow grazing near the forest. After their attack, the lion suddenly became hostile and gave a loud, frightening roar. The hyenas were afraid and one of them said, "We, the sons of the hyena, have never taken any living booty home. We always eat what is left over by you. You may take the nine bulls and we will take the old cow." With the lion's approval, the hyenas took the old cow home with them.

Their father, the old hyena, was patiently waiting for his sons to return. His sons placed the old cow in front of him and offered him how their greetings respectfully. The old hyena asked them how their hunting adventure had gone and his sons told him how they met the lion and attacked nine bulls and the old cow together. They also told him how the lion frightened them and how they were forced into taking only the old cow out of the fine lot.

The old hyena was outraged. "You are cowards and have disgraced me," he said. "You are nine in number, yet you allowed one lion to take away nine fine bulls we could have had. Instead, you have come back home with an old cow. I will take the old cow back to the lion and bring back home the nine bulls!" Having said this, the old hyena ordered his sons to take him where the lion was staying.

The old hyena and his sons arrived at the scene where the lion was feasting. The lion was angry at being interrupted from his happy meal and roared loudly. "Why do you come? What do you want?" His voice shook the air and made the nine young hyenas tremble. The old hyena looked into the lion's fiery eye, opened his mouth, closed it, opened his mouth again, and finally said, "I came to apologize about what these foolish sons of mine did. We are scavengers. We only eat the leftovers of what others have killed. You may as well take the old cow and feast on it as you have with the nine bulls."

So, the old hyena who had vowed to return home with the nine bulls gave away the old cow his sons had brought back to the lion. When the hyenas reached home, they were all tired and hungry.

Moral

One must not brag
of strength one does not have.

Ethiopia:

Ethiopia is a large country nestled on the northeast tip of Africa, surrounded by Somalia, Kenya, Uganda, Sudan, and Eritrea. Influenced by ancient Egypt and Greece and, later, Arab traders and explorers, Ethiopia has a rich cultural history. Today, its diverse people live alongside the ruins of ancient palaces and temples. CARE is helping many poor Ethiopians to improve their lives by teaching them better health and nutrition practices and how to improve their communities through food-for-work exchanges.

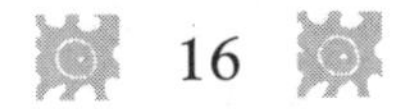

KENYA

The Chemosit: A Nandi Tale

by Bibi Dina Jepkemboi

A long time ago, near the forest of Nandi Land, there lived a family of three: a father, a mother, and their eight-year-old son, Kibet.[1] The family had many cattle to tend, so every morning the father and mother took the cattle to graze

1 Rhymes with Ti-*bet*.

in the grasslands, which were far away. They left early in the morning with the cattle and didn't return until evening.

The boy was left at home alone because he couldn't walk that far. His parents told him to lock the door from inside and not to unlock it until he heard his mother's voice in the evening singing this song:

> Kibet, oh, Kibet; Kibet, oh, Kibet.
> Yot-wo kur-get oh Kibet oh ka-ko-it Mama.
> Kibet, oh, Kibet; Kibet, oh, Kibe-e-et.[2]

So this is how they made sure their boy was safe. The boy knew the voice of his mama very well, and he knew what time his parents returned with the cattle each evening. Both parents were sure a stranger could not get to Kibet, because he would not open the door for any stranger.

Meanwhile, in the forest nearby, there lived a Chemosit,[3] a monster who eats children. The Chemosit had been watching and knew that the boy was home alone waiting to hear his mother's song each evening.

One day after the parents had left, Chemosit went to the boy's house, stood at the door, and started to sing in a rough voice:

2 Tune included at end of story.
3 Sounds like *Chem*-o-seat.

Kibet, oh, Kibet; Kibet, oh, Kibet.
Yot-wo kur-get oh Kibet oh ka-ko-it Mama.
Kibet, oh, Kibet; Kibet, oh, Kibe-e-et.

The voice sounded so bad that Kibet knew right away this was not his mama's.

Chemosit went home mad because he didn't get the boy. But then he practiced and practiced to sound more like the boy's mama.

That evening, when his parents returned, Kibet told them that he had heard the Chemosit singing but had not opened the door. The boy's parents were pleased and proud of him.

The next day Chemosit came back. He sang the song, and again Kibet knew this was not his mama. The voice was too deep. Besides, his parents never came home so early.

Now Chemosit became really upset. He went home again and didn't sleep that night. He kept thinking of how he could trick the boy. Finally he remembered hearing about a bird called Chepchenge,[4] whose work was to shape voices to sound the way people want them to sound.

"I can't wait to see that bird," Chemosit said to himself. He fell asleep thinking of the boy and he

4 Sounds like Chep-*chen*-geh (hard "g").

dreamed of how delicious the boy would taste. When he woke up, Chemosit walked deep into the forest searching for Chepchenge.

The Chepchenge bird was basking in the morning sun when she heard a rough voice calling, "Chepchenge! Chepchenge!"

The bird answered, "Hello, there. How are you today?"

Chemosit told the bird that he wanted her to make his voice sweet. When the bird asked, "Why?" Chemosit replied, "So I can sing to my wife."

The bird was so impressed that she didn't realize Chemosit was lying. Chemosit knew that if he had told Chepchenge the truth, the bird would have refused to shape his voice.

The bird started to get busy. "How would you like your voice to sound?" Chemosit told her, and in an hour Chemosit's voice sounded exactly as he wished, just like the boy's mama.

When she had finished, Chepchenge said, "You may go now. But remember: Don't eat anything all day." Chemosit promised, and off he went.

On the way to the boy's house, Chemosit saw a fly wandering by and he ate it. He kept right on walking until he stood outside the boy's door and started to sing:

Kibet, oh, Kibet; Kibet, oh, Kibet.
Yot-wo kur-get oh Kibet oh ka-ko-it Mama.
Kibet, oh, Kibet; Kibet, oh, Kibe-e-et.

But his voice sounded more horrible than before! It was too deep and more rough than you can imagine! The boy, of course, didn't open the door. He called out, "I'm not stupid, you know."

Chemosit was so disappointed as he headed back to the forest. That evening the boy's parents came home at the usual time, and Kibet told them what had happened. They hugged him and told him he was very clever for not being fooled by that stranger.

In the morning, Chemosit went back to see the bird Chepchenge.

"Well, well, what do you want now?" asked Chepchenge.

"Sorry, I ate a fly," replied Chemosit.

The bird laughed for a long time, then said, "Aren't you ashamed? A big creature like you eating a little fly? Well, I will shape your voice again if you promise not to eat anything all day." Chemosit promised. Chepchenge shaped his voice and told him to go.

As Chemosit was walking toward the boy's house he passed a mosquito and gobbled it down. When he reached Kibet's door and began to sing, his voice

was so high, and whined so, that again the boy was not fooled.

Chemosit went home so mad with himself, promising that next time he would follow the rules and get that boy for sure.

In the morning, Chemosit again went to Chepchenge. This time the bird didn't laugh. "This is the last time, and don't come back ever again. I don't want to see your face anymore." She shaped his voice and told him to get lost. Chemosit left, and this time made sure he didn't eat anything at all.

When Chemosit reached the boy's house, he began singing in a beautiful voice:

Kibet, oh, Kibet; Kibet, oh, Kibet.
Yot-wo kur-get oh Kibet oh ka-ko-it Mama.
Kibet, oh, Kibet; Kibet, oh, Kibe-e-et.

At that same time the boy's parents had started toward home. As the Chemosit's song continued, the boy said to himself, "That's my mama's voice, but what is she doing home so early?"

Chemosit kept singing. He sang and sang.

When the parents reached the top of the hill where they could see their home, they also saw the Chemosit standing in front of their home. They started to run with all their strength.

As the Chemosit sang on and on, the boy at last opened the door! Chemosit grabbed him up and was about to swallow him down when the parents arrived.

"Stop! Don't touch our son!" they yelled. Chemosit turned. When he saw it was the boy's parents, he jumped one big jump over their heads and ran toward the river. The parents chased the monster all the way to the river. They saw him try to jump across the swift and powerful rapids. As Chemosit jumped, the boy squirmed free and fell to the bank, where he scrambled to his parents' waiting arms.

The Chemosit landed in the middle of the swirling waters. He screamed, "Shaaaash, shaaaaash!" Then he drowned, "Glup, glup, glup."

And that is why, to this day, when you go to the flooded river, you will hear "Shaaaash, shaaaaash! Glup, glup, glup."

So, children, don't go to the river without your parents, because the Chemosit just might jump out and grab you. And parents, no matter how clever and smart and obedient your children are, don't leave them home alone.

The Song:

quickly and with lightness
Ki - bet, oh Ki - bet; Ki - bet, oh Ki - bet
Yot-wo Kur-get oh Ki - bet oh Ka-koit Ma ma
[trans.–Open the door for me. Mama is here.]
Ki - bet, oh Ki - bet; Ki - bet, oh Ki - be-e-et

KENYA:

What do you think of when you think of Kenya? Lions, of course! This East African country is famous for its wildlife, such as lions, giraffes, elephants, and zebras. It is also famous for its beautiful and diverse countryside—including the foothills of the world-famous Mount Kilimanjaro. For twenty-seven years CARE has worked in Kenya, helping improve family health and pioneering agricultural programs that help people grow more and better food. In addition, CARE publishes a special children's magazine that teaches Kenyan youngsters the value of good health and nutrition, and shows them how to preserve the environment.

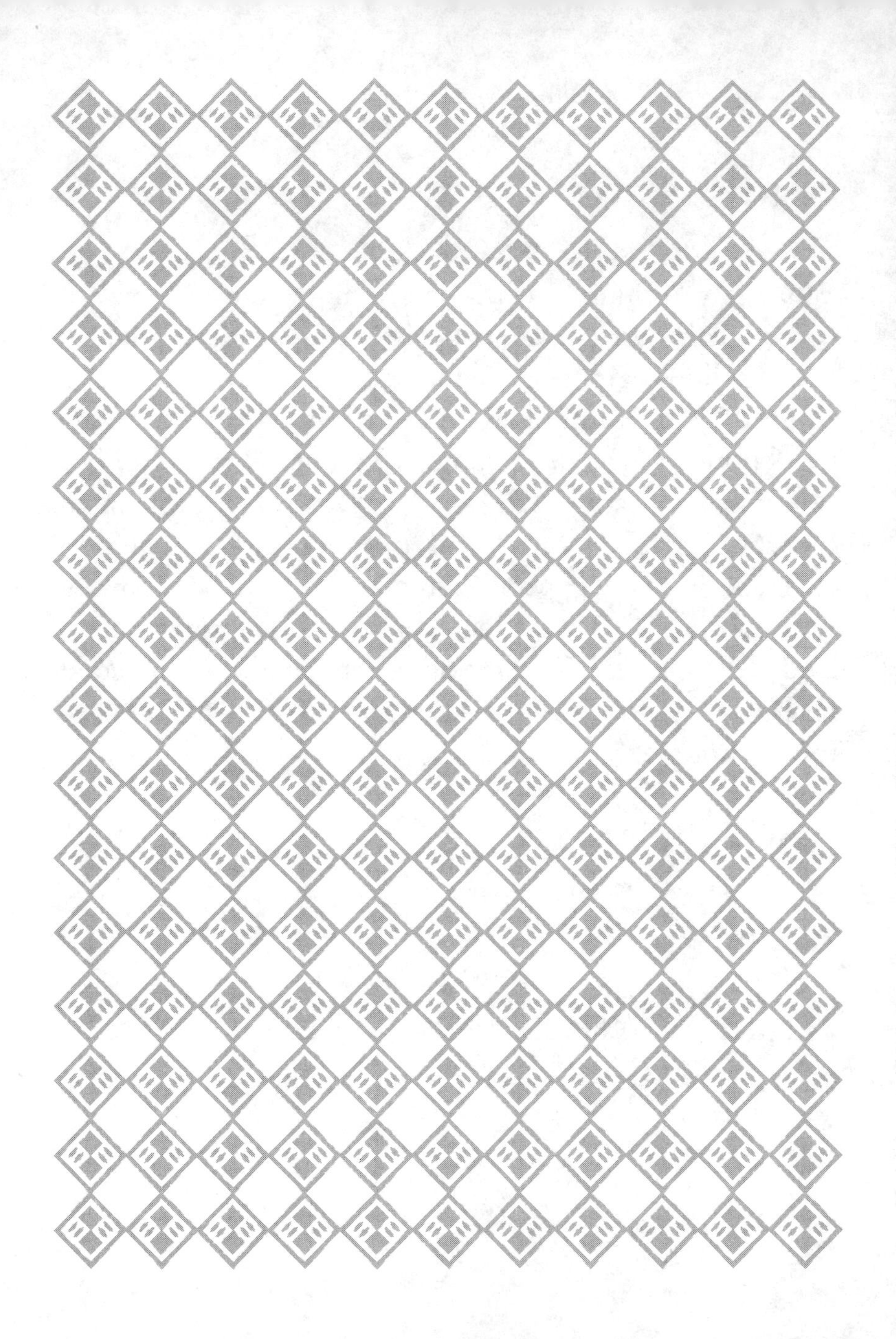

Wag

by Caroliese I. Frink Reed

A long time ago, there lived a great and brave hunter named Wag, who feared nothing. Wag was always the first to lead a hunt and the last to return, with many, many animals killed.

All of the villagers knew of and respected Wag, and many of the village's children aspired to grow up to be mighty hunters like Wag. Even people in the surrounding villages knew of Wag and often referred to him as the "Great Hunter."

All of the animals in the forest knew of Wag, too—for he was the most feared man-animal alive and a great threat to them. Each year their numbers grew smaller, and finally several of the animals banded the others together for a meeting to discuss what could be done to stop the killing of their kind.

One suggestion was for all of the animals to move to another forest, but most were against this idea, as the forest they now lived in had been theirs and their ancestors' home for centuries. Another suggestion was to make a fence from the limbs of baobab trees and hide behind it when the hunters were near, but it was pointed out that the dogs would be able to smell them even if they hid from sight.

Finally, a beautiful and sleek leopard stepped forward into the inner circle of animals and spoke: "It is the one named Wag who leads the others into the hunts; if we can stop Wag from wanting to hunt, then the others will follow."

The crowd of animals buzzed with agreement, but also with questions of how this could be done. The leopard said that she would allow herself to be turned into a beautiful woman; and the next time Wag came hunting with his many dogs, he would find her on the path alone and take her home with him. Once in his home, she would convince him to do things other than hunting.

All of the animals agreed that this was a good plan and they set it into motion. The leopard journeyed along the easternmost part of the rubble-covered Dogo hills, where there was a magic spring-fed well, kept secret since the beginning of time from the man-animals. She drank from the well, closed her eyes, and made her wish. When she opened her eyes, she saw the reflection of human eyes staring back at her in the springwater. "Oh my!" she said aloud; it was her staring back. Her wish was granted and she was no longer a leopard, but a beautiful woman with long dark hair and soft bronze skin.

The next day she went down by the river, where Wag had often taken his hunters, and sat patiently until he arrived later that afternoon. Wag asked her who she was and what circumstances had brought her to be sitting where she was, deep in the woods and far away from any village. She told him that she did not remember anything and he offered to take her home to live with his mother and him.

Once home, the mother took her in and made a bed for her. Soon Wag fell in love with her and they were married. All was well in the household, except that the new wife had very odd eating habits. All she ever asked her husband to bring her was meat—dog meat.

At first, this did not present a great problem for Wag, for he had many dogs. He was able to provide her with fresh dog meat every day. She prepared and cooked the meat, placing the bones in a jar. Wag's mother thought that this behavior was very strange and watched her new daughter-in-law very carefully. Wag also hunted less and less as the months went by because of the time that he now spent with his wife. His mother knew this was not good and feared for him.

Wag killed his dogs, one by one, until there were only his three favorite dogs left, Wala Ni, Wala Kani, and Wala Atemi. These three dogs had been with him the longest and were the most faithful. He hated to kill these three, but he loved his wife and she seemed to thrive only on dog meat.

When the last dog had been killed, Wag's wife said, "Come, let us go hunting together." Wag, although sad over the loss of his dogs, agreed, because in his heart, he was still a brave hunter.

So they both set off hunting together and soon came to a clearing near the river. Suddenly his wife began to make strange animal sounds the like of which he had never before heard. From the bush came rumblings and grumblings and roars, and soon he and his wife were

encircled by many different animals. Wag became frightened and pulled at his wife's hand to run to the tree in the center of the clearing. But she refused and pulled herself away, to stand with the animals crouched and ready for attack.

Wag ran to the tree and climbed up to its top, where he felt a light, cold rain which made him shiver. How he wished he had his favorite dogs, Wala Ni, Wala Kani, and Wala Atemi with him. He began to cry out their names into the sky.

At home, Wag's mother felt something wrong in the air. She listened to the wind and heard the distant wails of her son. She ran to get the jar of bones and filled it with water. She shook and shook the jar and threw it out the door. On the ground, the bones wiggled and then began to move. They formed the shapes of three skeletons. The wind grew in might and the rain fell harder. And, as the storm worsened, the shapes of Wala Ni, Wala Kani, and Wala Atemi formed on the skeletons. Suddenly the wind and rain died down and the three dogs went wild, yelping and growling and sniffing around for Wag's scent.

Once the three enchanted dogs picked up the hunter's scent, they ran straight for the clearing by the river and attacked the animals. They killed all but the leopard-woman, who appeared human, but then they recognized the deception of her enchantment. They began to stalk her, but Wag from up in the tree yelled, "Wait!" He climbed down and made the dogs keep their distance. He marched up to his wife and demanded to know why she and the other animals had planned this trap for him.

She said, "You are a brave hunter, but you have killed many of my kind. There are not many left. We wish to live in peace and harmony like the man-animals."

For the first time Wag had known the feeling of being the hunted rather than the hunter. He promised to stop hunting and asked her to remain his wife. She agreed.

Wag called his dogs to his side and whispered something in their ears. Then he clapped his hands together and the dogs began to run from one animal to another, licking the wounds that had left them dead. Before their eyes, the animals' wounds healed and they arose, alive again! Wag and his wife left with the dogs for home, and for all of their years together after, the animals were welcome visitors at their residence.

MALI:

Tucked within the sweltering Sahara desert, Mali is a huge West African nation of rolling dunes and grassy plains. Its capital city is Bamako, but Mali is perhaps best known for the legendary city of Timbuktu—in ancient times a center of trade and Islamic study. Today, Mali still struggles with its historic enemy: drought. To help with this problem, CARE runs farming and irrigation programs to improve crops, and in time of famine distributes food and other relief supplies. CARE also teaches Mali's villagers about good health and nutrition.

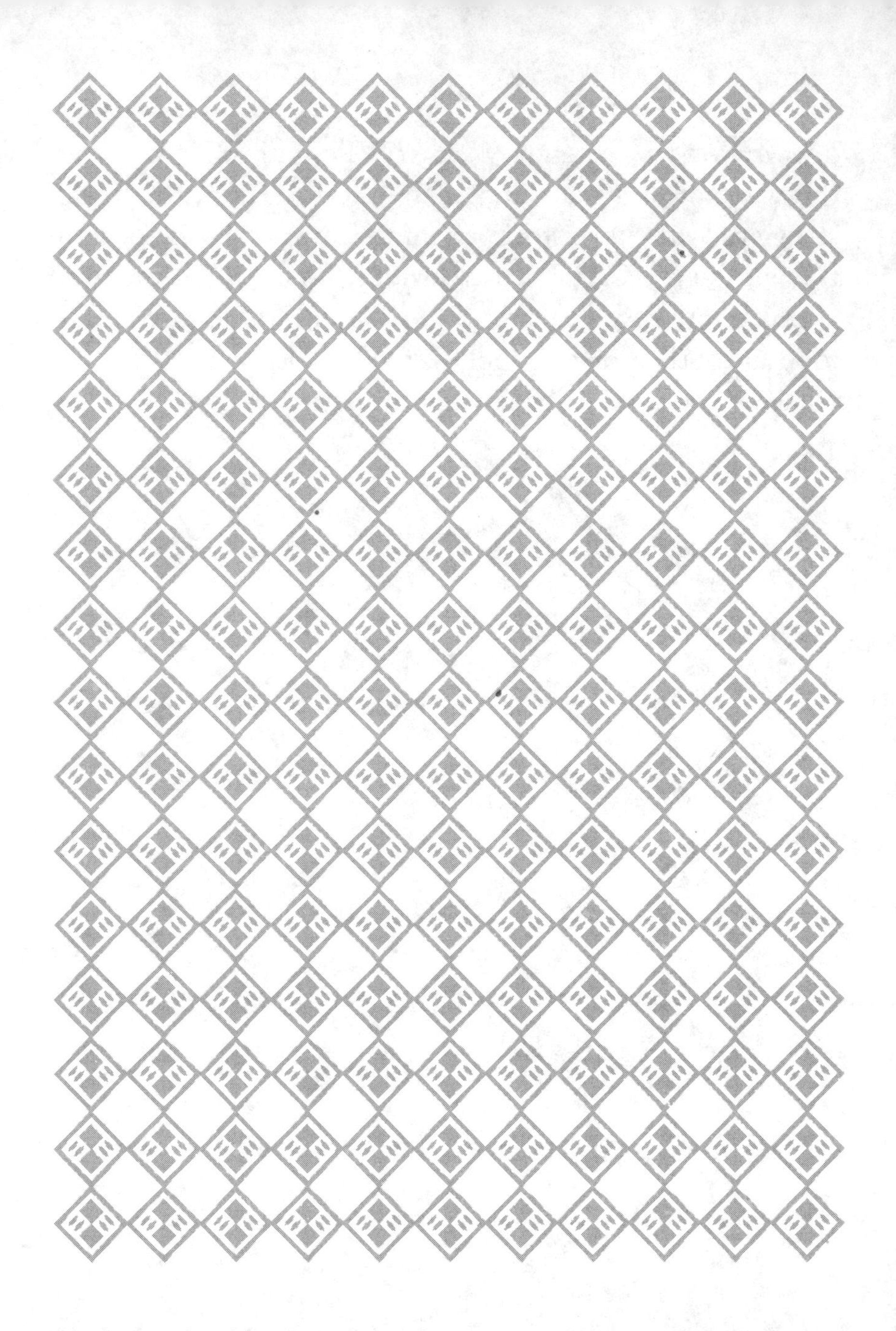

NIGERIA

The Blind Man's Stolen Cows

by Paul Newman

A very long time ago, there was a man of modest means whom God helped to become rich and prosperous like a Fulani. In the beginning, this man had started with just a few cows, but as time passed his farm grew to be the largest in the region. But sadly, the man also began to lose his eyesight little by little until he became completely blind and could no longer see his cows.

In this region, there also lived a very dishonest and greedy chief. Hearing the news that the old farmer had become blind, the chief realized that he now had a great opportunity to make himself richer. The chief decided to send his men to the blind man's farm one night.

While the blind farmer was asleep, the chief's men quietly rounded up all of his cows and stole away into the night. The blind man slept through the robbery. However, the chief's men were not even afraid that he would wake up. They knew that since he could not see, he would be completely helpless.

The next morning, the blind man woke up, and went to the pens to feed his many beloved cows. He discovered that he had been robbed. Devastated, he cried and weeped bitterly. A strong and determined man, the blind farmer decided he would go and search for the robbers and his cows.

The blind man left his home and went down the road tapping his stick, steering himself in the direction the robbers had led away his cows. After he walked for a few miles, his stick hit a tree stump. The stump greeted the blind man, and said, "Old man, where are you going?"

The blind man replied, "Some people came during the night when I was asleep and they have stolen all my cows. I am now searching for them."

Feeling very sorry for the blind man, the tree stump offered, "Please, I want to help. May I come along with you?"

The blind farmer said, "Yes. Bless you."

So the tree stump uprooted itself from the ground, and walked alongside the blind farmer as he continued tapping his stick.

Along the way, they met a cattle egret who had swooped down from the sky to catch a worm he had seen crawling along the road. After swallowing his lunch, the egret greeted the blind man and the tree stump, and asked, "Where are you going?"

The stump replied, "Someone has stolen this blind man's cows. So we are trying to find the robbers and the cows."

The egret then asked, "Please, I want to help. May I come along with you? Since I have eyes, I will be of great assistance to help spot the footprints of the robbers and cows."

The blind man said, "Yes. Bless you."

The egret then flew up and perched himself on the blind man's shoulder, and off the three of them went. "Tap, tap, tap," went the blind man's stick.

After a while, the blind man and his two friends met a wild pig. The pig of course greeted them and asked, "Where are you going?"

The blind man replied, "My cows have been stolen and we are searching for them."

The pig then said, "Please, I want to help. May I come along with you? Since I have a big snout, I will be of great assistance since I will be able to sniff the scent of the robbers and cows."

"Yes. Bless you," said the blind man.

So the wild pig joined the trio, and as they walked some more, they met a tsetse fly.

The tsetse fly asked, "Where are you going?"

The blind man again replied, "My cows have been stolen and we are trying to find them."

The tsetse fly then said, "Please, I want to help. May I come along with you?"

"Yes. Bless you," said the blind man.

The blind man and his four friends continued walking, following the trail of the robbers and his cows. Finally, they were led into the town where the chief resided.

The stump, the egret, the wild pig and the tsetse fly came upon the townspeople and asked, "Have you seen this blind man's cows? They were taken from him during the night and we have followed their trail all the way into this town."

The townspeople replied, "Yes. They are in our chief's pens," not knowing that their chief had actually stolen the cows.

Several of the chief's men had overheard the conversation between the townspeople and the blind man and his friends. They immediately ran to their chief with this news. "Indeed, our townspeople have told the blind man and his friends that you have his cows. What shall we do? We do not want your subjects to know that you have stolen this poor blind man's cows."

The chief, who was now very scared about what his subjects' reaction would be if they were to discover the truth, said, "Why not take the cows and give them back, saying we found them lost along the road?"

The chief's councilor, who was even a more dishonest and greedy man than his chief, said, "No, we cannot simply let the cows go like that. Let us make a plan. We shall kill the blind man and his friends, and then the cows will become forever yours."

The chief nodded in agreement and said, "All right, it will be done your way."

The councilor went to greet the visitors and offered to lodge them in the chief's guest house. The councilor led the guests to their quarters and said, "The chief hopes your stay will be a most enjoyable one. Since you must be very tired from your journey, he has arranged for you to be served a wonderful meal tonight. Please let me know if you will need anything else." He left the quarters to return to the chief.

The tsetse fly was somewhat suspicious of the chief's wonderful hospitality and said to his companions, "Wait for me here until I return." He flew off, and landed on the councilor's robe and hid in its folds.

The councilor went to meet the chief at court. The councilor said, "Chief, we have lodged our guests."

The chief asked, "But what will we do?"

The councilor replied, "Order your cooks to mix the strongest of poisons into the food that is being prepared for them right now. When they eat it, they will surely die. And then the cows will become forever yours."

The chief nodded and said, "It will be done like that, councilor."

The councilor then bowed out, and the tsetse fly who had heard the whole conversation flew off quickly to warn his companions.

The tsetse fly recounted the councilor's evil plot. "But I cannot do anything more to help since I am nothing but a speck of a fly."

The tree stump said, "Do not worry. Let them come with the food. Let God just bring them."

The blind man and his friends waited for the chief's servant to bring their food. The chief had ordered plenty of food to be cooked and ensured that plenty of poison was mixed into it. All the food was piled high onto one big dish. As the tree stump saw the servant carrying the huge plate of food, he quickly got up and squatted in his pathway. The servant tripped over the stump and fell to the ground. The poisoned food splattered onto the ground and the dish broke into a thousand pieces. The tree stump returned to his companions.

The servant returned to his chief and explained the accident.

The chief admonished the servant for not being more careful, and said, "All right, just leave it at that. We will wait until tomorrow morning."

The next morning, the councilor, pretending to be very friendly, went to greet the blind man and his friends. He then returned to his chief with a different plan. Again, the tsetse fly went along, hiding in the folds of his robe.

The chief said to the councilor, "As you know, our plan failed. Why do we not just give them back the cows and we can be rid of them?"

The councilor said, "Chief, all is not over as of yet. I have another plan. Tonight, when they are asleep, we shall send our men to set their quarters on fire. We will lock their doors and they will have no means of escape. Once they are dead, the cows will be forever yours."

The chief again said, "All right, it will be done like that."

The tsetse fly quickly returned to his friends to say, "They are going to set our quarters on fire tonight, and hope to burn and kill us."

The wild pig then said, "Do not worry. Let them come. God will save us."

During the evening, the wild pig dug a tunnel in their quarters leading to the outside of the house. The blind man, the tree stump, the egret and the tsetse fly escaped through the tunnel along with the pig, as the chief's men set the guest quarters on fire.

The next morning, the chief's men came to look at the torched remains, and to their surprise, found the blind man and his friends safe and sound, standing next to the hot glowing embers.

Astonished, the chief's men ran back and recounted what they had seen. "Indeed, these people, we cannot defeat them. They are there. They did not die."

The chief suddenly felt very, very discouraged, and said to his councilor, "My beautiful guest quarters have been burned to a pile of ashes. I told you that we should have just given them back their cows. Now, let us do so and be rid of them forever."

The councilor begged the chief to give him another chance. "I have one more plan. We shall catch them in a crime and have them imprisoned. Put all the cows, the stolen ones and yours into one pen, to mix them all up. Ask the blind man to go fetch his own cows. The only way to identify cows is by their color markings. Because he is blind, this will be an impossible task. However, since you will be able to do so, you can then rightfully accuse him of stealing your cows."

The tsetse fly flew back and recounted to his friends the councilor's latest plot.

The egret said, "Do not worry, I have a plan. God will help us."

The next morning, the councilor came to the blind man and told him, "The chief wishes to return your cows. You can go to the pen and take the ones that belong to you. However, you must absolutely make sure that the cows you take are yours."

The egret went along with the blind man. Perched on the blind man's shoulder, he whispered into his ear, "Tell me what are the color markings of your cows. I will do my best to seek them out. Once I have identified them, I will call you and you will then lead them out of the pen."

The job was easy. Once the blind man and his friends collected all his cows, the chief arrived to accuse them of theft. To his total astonishment, none of his cows had been taken out of the pens.

The blind man then asked simply, "Is this all finished? Are we allowed to leave now?"

Completely defeated, the chief and his councilor both said, "Yes, it is finished. Go on your way."

So, the blind man and his friends herded the cows and set back along the road to his farm many miles outside the town. The blind man rewarded his faithful friends for their help, and then headed home and herded his cows into their pens.

NIGERIA:

Located on the south coast of West Africa, Nigeria is a land of stunning contrasts. Its 356,000 square miles include a coastal mangrove swamp, a tropical rain forest, a wide plateau of grassy savanna and a semi-desert region in the north. Huge deposits of valuable oil are just one of this country's many riches. Another is the sprawling Niger river, which has tributaries extending like a dense web across this fertile African country. In recent years, population growth, poverty and political instability have combined to threaten Nigeria's people and environment. CARE provided food and supplies for Nigerians during the Biafran Civil War and an ensuing famine.

TOGO

The Two Hunters

by Tchedre Safiou

Once upon a time, there were two hunters who were very good friends. They always hunted together and had done so since they were little boys. Whenever they went out hunting, they went as brothers, sharing everything equally between them.

This was their arrangement and it held for many years.

One day they went hunting far away from their homes for many days without finding any game to kill. So they searched the woods and dug yams and cooked them to stay alive. They lived on these sweet and meaty roots for many more days and continued to hunt without any reward.

One morning they came upon a huge rock and climbed up to its crest. There, they found a bird's nest with two eggs. Well, the hunting was so bad that they each took one egg and headed back to their homes.

Back home, one hunter cooked his egg and ate it. The other kept and nurtured his for nine months and his egg hatched two children: a boy and a girl. He raised the two children, and now that he had new responsibilities and children to rear, he no longer hunted with his friend.

Years passed and the two friends had not seen or hunted with one another. One day the friend who had saved his egg came to visit his old hunting companion, sad that they had not been together in so many years. The friends were very glad to see one another. They ate fresh fruit and drank sweet juice and talked many hours into the night.

Eventually, the visitor asked of the other: "What did you do with your egg?"

The host replied happily, "I ate it and it tasted so good."

The first continued: "As for me, I kept mine and it has given me two children."

His friend did not believe him and grew angry at such a farce—how dare his friend mock him so with such a story! They argued, but to no avail. The visitor went back home to his children.

A year later, the friend who had eaten his egg came to call upon his old hunting companion. He wanted to see these so-called children for himself, even though he didn't believe the story.

When he arrived, he was greeted by two children and again grew very angry at his friend, insisting that he have one of the children, as they had always shared what they had found. They argued and argued and finally went to God to render judgment on this affair.

The friend who ate his egg exclaimed: "We had an agreement to share half of everything we found on our hunting expeditions equally. It was always that way."

The friend who saved his egg agreed, explaining: "Yes, indeed we had that agreement. So much is true. And we found two eggs and each took one home. At the time what we had found had been divided equally."

God listened to both of the friends' accounts and finally spoke unto them: "I must agree with the one who saved his egg. Had the other saved his egg as well, he would most likely have two children of his own now. The two children belong to the one who had them bestowed upon him. To the other belongs the memory of a tasty egg. I have spoken."

The two friends separated, the one who had eaten his egg more angry than ever. Rather than making peace with his old friend, he stubbornly searched for many years for another egg that would bear him children, but alas, he never found one. Disappointed and saddened, he disappeared in his loneliness, never to be heard from again. The friend who saved his egg lived a long life with his two children caring for him.

A thin sliver of land bordering the Atlantic Ocean in West Africa, Togo is a tiny but fertile country. Its chief crops include coffee, yams, manioc, millet, rice, and the cocoa beans that are used to make hot chocolate. CARE is helping this poor country to improve its farmland and preserve the environment through tree-planting and agroforestry programs. CARE also teaches Togolese people better health, helps them to start their own small businesses, and teaches AIDS prevention.

Asian Stories

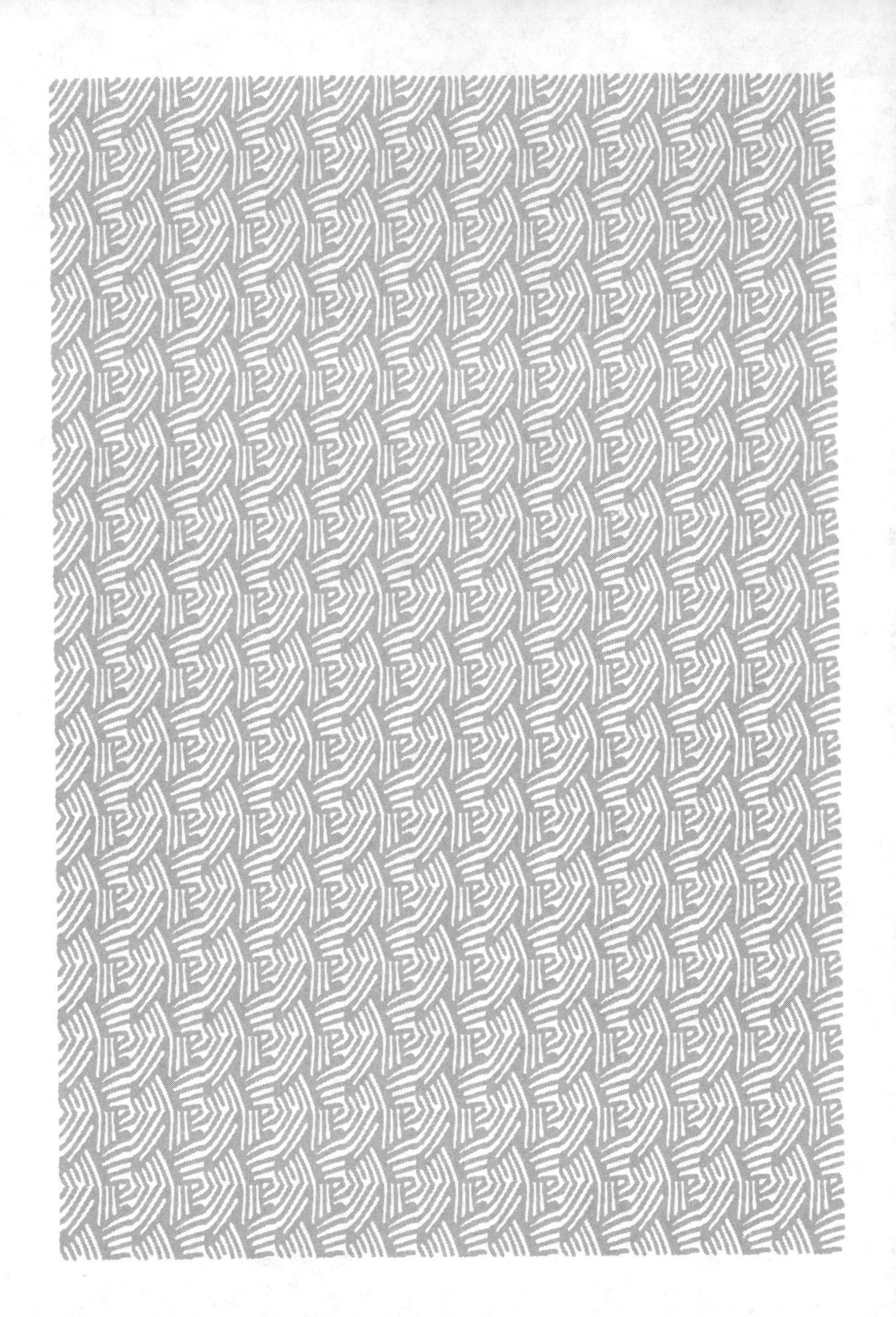

Kanchan Mala

by Kaiser Parvez Ali

Once upon a time, in a faraway distant kingdom, there lived a noble king and queen who had an only son named Neel Manik. He was a handsome and intelligent boy and all of the Kingdom's subjects bestowed upon him the highest of praises. The young women of the Kingdom ogled him whenever he walked by, as he frequented the city shops, but none could capture his notice.

As the Prince grew up and became of an age when he was eligible for marriage, the King and Queen sent couriers to other kingdoms, near and far, to search for a suitable match for their son. But alas, it seemed that none was worthy of the Prince's affections. This troubled the young Prince, who wanted a mate, but also wanted to please his parents and abide by their wishes.

One day the Prince was on a hunting expedition in the outer reaches of the Kingdom lands, something he often did to pass the time and to take his mind off of his marital predicament. Prince Neel Manik loved to hunt birds, scouring the countryside with bow and arrow in hand to search for all kinds. In the entire Kingdom, there were none to match his skill in the hunt of winged creatures. However, this day, he was unsuccessful in his hunt. Feeling disappointed and dejected, he sat down under a branch of a tree to rest.

Suddenly a small bird of extraordinary grace and beauty alighted on the branch above him and spoke: "My name is Heera Mon, I know that you are looking for a bride. There is one princess in a place called Sonar Moti Jaler Dule. Her name is Kanchan Mala and she is in a deep sleep, surrounded and closely guarded by demons. If you can find her and rescue her from her frightful fate, she will awaken to marry you and you will be a very happy man."

Prince Neel Manik, who was used to hunting birds, put an arrow to his bow; this was to be his prize catch. But the bird saw what he was up to and quickly flew up into the sky and out of range as the arrow was released. The Prince thought hard about the bird's words and decided he would believe them. This was perhaps because it was the first prey to escape his arrow. The Prince wrapped his bow over his shoulder and embarked on the journey to Sonar Moti Jaler Dule to find the Princess.

He traveled for many days and nights, resting very little. All he could think of was how much his bride-to-be must be suffering and how much she needed of him.

One day the Prince came upon a tree, much like the one where he had met the bird. He found an old hermit sitting cross-legged with his eyes closed. As the Prince approached, the hermit opened his eyes and asked: "What do you want?"

The Prince replied, "I would like to find the Princess Kanchan Mala. Can you help me?"

The hermit's expression turned dark with foreboding and concern. He said: "The Princess lives across the

seven seas and thirteen rivers. It is a very dangerous place surrounded by demons far worse than you can imagine. You do not want to go there." The hermit closed his eyes.

The Prince prodded him and insisted, "But I must go there to see her and rescue her from sleep. She is to be my princess bride."

The hermit opened his eyes once again, measuring the Prince with his stare, an unusual thing for a hermit to do and especially to a royal prince. "Indeed your cause is just, Prince. If you are to go, I will give you the means to do so. For although my appearance is that of a hermit, a wizard once was I."

With a wave of his hand and the recital of an enchantment, the once wizard hermit turned the Prince into a bird. The Prince was outraged! He protested, squawking and hopping about. "I hunt birds. I will not be one!" he cried.

The hermit wizard, now towering over the little bird, spoke with a firmness and strength that took the Prince by surprise: "With this disguise, you will be able to fly into the Kingdom to rescue the Princess. It is the only way you will succeed."

"Change me into a hare; I will be swift and silent," the Prince offered.

"A moat surrounds the dark castle and a hare cannot swim," the hermit wizard said, now folding his arms.

"Then a horse, and I will get a guard to ride me into the castle," the Prince offered.

"Horses are kept in stables outside the castle, never allowed inside," the wizard hermit replied.

After a while, when all of the options the Prince could think of were exhausted, he acquiesced and agreed to be a bird. It was the only way to rescue the Princess.

The wizard hermit again spoke. "Once inside the castle walls, you will find the Princess in the castle keep. You must then land on her forehead and peck her cheek once to awaken her. Only then will she turn into a bird like you sc that you will be able to fly back to me again, together."

So the Prince flew over the seven seas and the thirteen rivers until finally he saw the castle below. What might have once been a majestic castle of stone was now overgrown with evil-looking vines that choked the sunlight from the castle windows. Neel Manik found the keep and the Princess, whom he found truly beautiful to behold. He landed gracefully onto her forehead and bent his feathery body over her face, pecking her lightly on the cheek. Instantly, she changed into the most beautiful and colorful bird he had ever seen! He spoke to her in a tweeting whisper: "I am Prince Neel Manik and have come to rescue you and take you home to my kingdom to be my wife."

She replied in a trilling voice, "I am forever yours, Prince Neel Manik, though you be a bird."

"But I am not a bird, I am—" he began as the door latch came undone. "Away, we must fly now!" he chirped, and they flew out of the keep window into the sky.

Once they were a safe distance from the castle walls, they landed on a tall tree overlooking the valley to rest. Suddenly an arrow wizzed by, frightfully close. In fact, Prince Neel Manik felt its wind against his feathers. "What are you doing?" the Princess yelled to the fool below while he prepared another arrow.

Befuddled, the young man gazed up at the birds who were really a prince and princess. "Did you speak?" the hunter asked.

"Why do you shoot at us? We have done nothing to harm you," the Princess said indignantly.

"That may be true," the hunter said, still confused and obviously frightened by the magic, "but I am the greatest hunter of fowl in this valley and you are a prize indeed." With that he shot another arrow, this time hitting the wing of the Prince's bride, injuring her.

"You fool! We are not to be shot at. I am the royal Prince Neel Manik and this is my princess bride!" The hunter pulled another arrow, but before he could shoot it, Princess Kanchan Mala climbed upon the Prince and they flew upward into the deep blue sky.

They flew all day and all night. By the dawn of the next morning, they came upon the tree where the wizard hermit sat. They landed upon a branch above the wizard hermit's head and he opened his eyes and looked up.

The Prince recounted the story of their escape from the castle keep and from the crazy hunter who sought their demise. The wizard hermit grinned and, with the wave of his hand and a brief incantation, changed the Prince and Princess back into human forms. The wizard handed the Prince his bow and arrows and spoke a second incantation as he turned from his human form into that of a bird.

The Prince smiled and said: "I welcome you into my kingdom at any time you may wish to visit Heera Mon. With these arrows I shall not hunt the winged creatures again."

The bird nodded its head and lifted into the sky, never to be seen again. The Prince and the Princess made their way back to the Kingdom and were married in luxurious splendor in the palace. The bird became the royal symbol from that day on and they lived happily ever after.

The lovely, grassy marshlands of this green country mask a hidden danger: the threat of deadly floods and typhoons during the rainy season. Since Bangladesh's wet climate and turbulent political history have put millions of families at risk, CARE has a big presence in the country. CARE offers food to poor Bangladeshis in return for help building roads and irrigation for farmland. CARE also offers agriculture and health care education, and was one of the first relief agencies to respond on a large scale when a devastating cyclone hit Bangladesh in the 1980s.

The Dishonorable Betrayal of Princess Jie Ming

by Eileen Wong

Many hundreds and hundreds of years ago, there lived a powerful and great Tang Chinese Emperor named Yin Lun. Of all the Tang Emperors, he was the most renowned and revered. Yin Lun had brought China to new heights of greatness. The Chinese Empire had become more vast than any Emperor could ever have dreamed. It stretched from the dry northern Mongolian desert plains to the tropical South China Seas, and from the huge western Tibetan mountains to the civilized eastern shores of Shanghai. While Yin Lun was a great warrior, he was also a lover of beauty. After many years of warfare, his empire now enjoyed peace and prosperity. And so, the great Tang Emperor mandated the building of beautiful palaces and cities, the writing of sublime poetry and literature, and the creation of the greatest Chinese dishes, among many other things. The Chinese Empire during Yin Lun's reign was not only the largest, but also the most beautiful and richest ever! China during this time was truly what he called "the center of heaven (中国)."

Yin Lun spent most of his time with his imperial court between his grand winter palace in Xian and his summer palace in Hangzhou. It was in Hangzhou, a city with the most wondrous mystical lake, that the Emperor met his tenth wife-to-be, the beautiful Princess Jie Ming. Yin Lun had never ever cast his eyes on anyone so pure and serene and bright (indeed, "bright" is exactly what the Princess's name meant in Chinese). During his courtship, he would say to the Princess as he looked deep into her bright, perfect and wide almond-shaped eyes, "Ah, my Jie Ming, your raven-black hair is like pure

Suzhou silk. Your skin is like the most delicate Chinese porcelain and your lips are the most deep red of a ripe cherry. You are truly wonderful!" However, what the Emperor loved most of all was her lyrical voice. When the Princess sang, it was like listening to the happiest Chinese sparrows.

Princess Jie Ming became the Emperor's favorite wife. Together, Yin Lun and the Princess had one son. "He shall be named Prince Wu Pin, son of the Kingdom of Heaven," proclaimed the Emperor. Yin Lun devoted most of his time to the Princess and his son when he was not dealing with state affairs. He built a small, beautiful palace alongside the mystical lake in Hangzhou, and an ornate apartment of imperial yellow for his tenth wife and son in his Xian winter palace. Since the Princess Jie Ming and her son were Yin Lun's most beloved possessions, he had golden dragon statues placed in front of their homes along with his most trusted and bravest imperial guards.

Princess Jie Ming loved her husband dearly. She took great pleasure in making the Emperor happy when he spent time with her and their son. However, the Princess had been very young when she married Yin Lun, and she felt that there was so much that she had not yet experienced or learned. He had not only married the most beautiful Princess in the whole

Chinese Empire, but he had married someone who was exceptionally bright and curious. Although Princess Jie Ming enjoyed singing immensely and it pleased her that Yin Lun took great pleasure in listening to her songs, she was not completely satisfied. The Princess felt very alone. The Emperor's other wives ostracized her, for they were insanely jealous, and the rest of the imperial court kept a safe and respectful distance from her since she was the most beloved possession of the Emperor. "I wish," Princess Jie Ming said with a sigh, "that I could just have someone to talk to, and could learn of the many things that there are in life."

Princess Jie Ming knew that her husband had been instrumental in promoting the now flourishing period of literature, music, fine art, and poetry in China. The Emperor was surrounded by the greatest scholars, writers, artists, statesman, and philosophers. One day Princess Jie Ming spoke to her husband. "Your Majesty," she said, "I wish to learn more about life. You have created such a wonderful kingdom, full of cultural richness, but I do not know any of this."

Yin Lun, who knew that his favorite wife was very smart and independent, did not want her to be unhappy. "My beautiful Princess, I understand. I will then mandate that you have the pick of the best imperial teachers in order to satisfy your heart's desire."

Princess Jie Ming was ecstatic. The Emperor gave her the best of the imperial court's teachers. She loved learning about Han poetry, Chinese philosophy, and best of all, Chinese painting. Princess Jie Ming felt that she was truly developing as a person as she enriched herself with these new ideas.

In the meantime the Emperor's nine other wives were seething with jealousy. Princess Jie Ming was not only the most beautiful but also the most intelligent among them. "*Ai ya!*" exclaimed the Old Queen, who was the most incensed. "How can this young nothing of a girl have such luxuries when she is the lowliest of Yin Lun's consorts, the number-ten wife! This is indeed a dishonor to us! How can she even request such privileges?"

During this time, much unrest was stirring in one of the Emperor's recently acquired provinces. Yin Lun's Supreme General was pacing back and forth in the winter palace's great hall as he told the Emperor of his great concerns. "Our imperial spies report that the rebel armies are rebuilding quickly," he announced. "The people of this province have felt terribly affronted since the day you took one of their favorite princesses, Jie Ming, for your wife. I think, Your Majesty, they will use this issue to start a war against us very soon."

Hearing this news, Yin Lun became furious. "How dare they!" he fumed. "General, start rounding up our best soldiers and horses. We will be prepared if they dare try to start with me again. I also want more guards to protect the Princess."

The General, however, replied, "But, Your Majesty, perhaps there is a better way to quell the situation. We have had so many years of warfare. Your citizens have enjoyed great peace and harmony for a long, long time. I would advise you to consider another solution. Perhaps we should return Princess Jie Ming to her homeland."

"Never!" roared Yin Lun. "Do not dispute with me."

The Old Queen overheard the Supreme General's discussion with the Emperor. "*Hao jie le!* How very good!" she exclaimed as she started to plot in her devious head. Later that day she accosted the Supreme General and persuaded him to join in her plan, a plan that would spare China warfare and lives. And for her, a plan that would get rid of Princess Jie Ming forever. "I could not help but overhear you express your concerns to the Emperor, Supreme General," said the Old Queen. "I, too, do not want to bring war again to this great empire. It will be better to return Princess Jie Ming to her homeland." And bending toward the Supreme General's ear, she whispered to him her plan.

When Yin Lun was told of how Princess Jie Ming had betrayed him with one of his young guards—for this,

indeed, was the Old Queen's plan—his wail could be heard throughout the halls of the winter palace. He was choked with shame and fury. He screamed in disbelief, "It cannot be that she would do such a thing. I, who have showered her with all the greatness and splendor of this kingdom. And this is how she pays me back!" He paced furiously up and down the great hall, with the tails of his imperial yellow robe whipping the air. He finally turned to the Supreme General and commanded, "Arrest her and my son. They will not even get the chance to be returned to her homeland. Their heads will hang in shame! They will be punished by death for this dishonor!" The Supreme General bowed to Yin Lun and went to order the arrest of Princess Jie Ming and her son.

One of the Princess's favorite and most beloved teachers overhead the Emperor's cries as he was walking through the palace's halls. He was incredulous. Professor Chu knew that Jie Ming could never be guilty of such a terrible act of betrayal. The wise Professor ran to the Princess's antechamber and found her there painting a beautiful scene of the mystical lake where she had first met the Emperor. Red in the face from his exertion and with great fear in his voice, he said, "Quickly, my honorable Princess. There is no time to talk. Just bring the young Prince to the Jade Garden Pond as soon as you

can." Jie Ming was bewildered and did not understand what this urgent request was about, but she trusted Professor Chu and did as he asked.

At the Jade Garden Pond, Professor Chu and a trusted guard who was sympathetic to the Princess's plight met the young royals. The four of them, disguised as Chinese peasants, took flight to the southern province of Guangzhou. They finally settled in the Tai Shan mountain area, a place where it would be very difficult for the Emperor to find them.

At first, when the Princess learned of the great misunderstanding and of the Emperor's fury, she wanted to return to explain to her husband and be redeemed, but wise Professor Chu convinced her that such an action would be futile. "There is nothing more powerful than the shame that has befallen your husband. He will never believe you. His Queen and Supreme General have affirmed this so-called truth to him," he explained to the Princess.

Deeply saddened, the Princess nevertheless accepted her fate. There was no hope of ever returning to the Emperor she had once loved and trusted. She knew that she was really the one who had been betrayed. Taking the sage advice of Professor Chu, she and her son adopted new identities in case Yin Lun ever came looking for them.

However, Jie Ming was still a very proud woman. As she raised her son on the new farm where she lived with Professor Chu and the ex-royal guard, she vowed that her son's royal birthright and heritage would never be forgotten. She said to her young son, "Remember, you are and will always be the son of a Chinese emperor. So you must promise me that you will record this honorable right in our family tombs upon my death. And that your descendants will carry this information into the many thousand years to come."

With the help of Professor Chu, she had herself and her son renamed with the esteemed family name of Wong. As she explained to the Prince, "This new name means 'king.' Always remember that you are the son of a Chinese emperor. This name will ensure that future generations will know that they are descended from you, Young Prince Wu Pin."

And so this was how the many Wongs of China came to flourish for many centuries afterward. Whoever bears the Wong character (王) will know this sad story of how a beautiful and independent princess was shamefully wronged, and how her son was denied his imperial rights. But he or she will also know and be proud that they are blue-blooded descendants of a Tang prince.

China:

The huge stone wall known around the world as the Great Wall of China has for centuries been used by this ancient culture to keep the world out. Inside the wall, however, one of the world's great civilizations was born, and the influence of the art, science, and culture of the Chinese can be seen around the world. Despite a rich history, China still has many poor regions and it is here that CARE works, providing health care to families and offering poverty-reduction projects. CARE was the first Western relief and development agency to operate in China.

The Monkey and the Crocodile

by Andrea Rodericks

There was once a monkey who lived in a rose-apple tree on the banks of a river. Even though Mr. Monkey lived all by himself, he was very happy. He had a pleasant nature, and would wave to all the passersby from his perch on the highest branch of the rose-apple tree. The tree was laden with fruit throughout most of the year, and was also home to many birds. Mr. Monkey would often throw some fruit down for the children as they went off to school. One day, as he was playing by himself, a huge crocodile slid out of the river and lay down on the banks to sun himself.

Seeing the crocodile, the monkey called out from his treetop, "Who are you?"

The crocodile looked up and saw the monkey peering at him through the branches. "I am Mr. Crocodile," he said. "I've come from far away, in search of food."

"Food? Why search for food?" asked Mr. Monkey. "Look at this tree. It is laden with rose apples. Have some, you are sure to enjoy them." With that, the monkey threw down some fruit.

The crocodile took one bite and exclaimed, "This is the best fruit I have ever eaten! Thank you, Mr. Monkey. May I visit again?"

Mr. Monkey was very friendly and enjoyed having other animals visit him. He said, "You are most welcome. Come again and have as many rose apples as you want." Mr. Crocodile promised to come again, and then slid off into the river.

Thus the monkey and crocodile became friends. Mr. Crocodile started coming to visit Mr. Monkey every day, and the two of them spent several hours together. They

would sit and talk about all their experiences while they ate the juicy rose apples. One day they spoke about their families. The monkey said that he was alone, and felt lucky to have a good friend like Mr. Crocodile. Mr. Crocodile explained that he lived on the other side of the riverbed with his wife. Mr. Monkey was surprised to hear that Mr. Crocodile was married. "Why did you not tell me earlier that you were married?" he asked. "I would have sent some rose apples to your home."

That day Mr. Crocodile went home with some rose apples for his wife. She thoroughly enjoyed them, so he promised to bring her some more the next day.

As time passed, the monkey and crocodile grew closer to each other, and began to spend more and more time together. Mr. Monkey would always send some rose apples home with Mr. Crocodile. Mrs. Crocodile relished the rose apples, but did not like Mr. Crocodile coming home late every day. One evening, when Mr. Crocodile returned, she asked him, "How is it possible that you spend all your time in the company of a monkey. I don't think you are telling me the truth."

Mr. Crocodile said, "It is true, dear, Mr. Monkey and I are great friends."

Mrs. Crocodile was not convinced. She said, "We crocodiles kill monkeys and eat them. It is not possible that you spend your time in the company of a monkey."

Again Mr. Crocodile tried to explain. "Mr. Monkey is my best friend. Every day we talk about life and everything we know. I have learned a great deal from him about this town, as he is able to see far from his perch on the tree. He is also very generous, and gives me rose apples to eat. He sends you some every day. I thought you would be pleased."

"Ah!" said Mrs. Crocodile. "If Mr. Monkey eats nothing but these rose apples, his flesh must be very juicy and sweet. I think he would make the most delicious dinner. If you are such good friends, why don't you invite him to our home one day. I would love to meet him."

"I don't think I could do that," said Mr. Crocodile. "You see, Mr. Monkey lives on land, and our home is at the bottom of the river. Besides, I don't even know if he can travel in water."

"That is not for you to worry about," said Mrs. Crocodile, annoyed that her husband was making excuses. "You just invite him. Monkeys are clever; I am sure he will find a way to visit us." Mr. Crocodile did not like the idea at all. He did not want his friend to come to any harm.

Days went by, and Mrs. Crocodile saw no signs of Mr. Monkey, but she was still eager to have him for dinner. Soon she could think of nothing else but juicy, sweet monkey flesh. She knew Mr. Crocodile had not made any effort to invite Mr. Monkey to their home, so she began to plan out a way she could arrange this herself.

One morning, when the crocodiles awoke, Mrs. Crocodile pretended to be very ill. She appeared to be in great pain and began to shed crocodile tears. Mr. Crocodile was very upset and did not know what to do to ease his wife's pain. "How can I help you, my dear?" he asked her.

"I am very ill," she said. "I spoke to our doctor, and he says I have a serious disease, which can only be cured if I eat a monkey's heart."

"A monkey's heart?" Mr. Crocodile exclaimed. "That is a strange cure. Are you sure that is what you must have?"

"Yes," said Mrs. Crocodile. "Hurry, there is not much time. This disease is very dangerous. You must get me Mr. Monkey's heart."

"I couldn't do that," said Mr. Crocodile. "Mr. Monkey is my best friend. I cannot harm him."

"Then why don't you go and live with Mr. Monkey!" said Mrs. Crocodile angrily. "You don't love me. The only one you think about is your friend Mr. Monkey. Go away!"

Now Mr. Crocodile began crying. "I cannot kill my only friend. I couldn't bear it if any harm came to him."

"Why can't you kill a monkey?" Mrs. Crocodile asked. "Crocodiles are supposed to kill monkeys. Now I know you don't love me at all. A wife cannot live without her husband's love. This evening when you return after visiting your friend, I will be no more."

Mr. Crocodile was in a fix. He loved his friend dearly, but he had always been taught that it was his duty to look after his wife and protect her from any harm. Now the only way he could save her life was by killing his best friend. Reluctantly, he went to visit Mr. Monkey.

Mr. Monkey was waiting for him. "Why are you late, my friend? Did you have any trouble on the way?" he said from the treetop.

"No," replied Mr. Crocodile. "No trouble on the way, but my wife and I quarreled this morning. She says that I am not your friend because you have been so good to us, and I have not even invited you to our home. My wife has instructed me to invite you over this evening. She is very eager to meet you."

"How sweet of your wife to invite me home," said Mr. Monkey. "I would also like to meet her, but I will drown if I try to go to your home. You live in water, and I have never learned how to swim."

"Don't worry," said Mr. Crocodile. "We live on the riverbank. I can take you across the river on my back."

Mr. Monkey was pleased with this solution. "I'm ready, let's go," he said, and climbed onto Mr. Crocodile's back. Mr. Crocodile began to swim across the river. Mr. Monkey was enjoying the ride until they reached the middle of the river and Mr. Crocodile began to dive down toward the riverbed. "Hey," cried Mr. Monkey. "What are you doing? Don't go down any farther. I cannot swim." Mr. Monkey was scared, and wished he had learned how to swim. "It's all very well to get up to tricks in the water, Mr. Crocodile, but I will drown," Mr. Monkey cried in fright.

"That is the idea," Mr. Crocodile announced. "I am going to drown you."

"Drown me?" said Mr. Monkey in total shock. "But why would you want to kill me?"

Mr. Crocodile explained. "You see, my wife is very ill; her life is in danger. The doctor says she must eat a monkey's heart as soon as possible. You are the only monkey I know, so I am going to give her your heart. It is my duty to save my wife's life."

Mr. Monkey was really scared now. Unless he thought of something very fast, he would die. Suddenly it came to him. "My good friend, Mr. Crocodile, why didn't you tell me that you wanted my heart," he said. "I would willingly give it to you to save your wife's life. But I'm afraid I cannot give it to you just now. You see, I keep it in a hole in the rose-apple tree for safekeeping. I forgot to bring it with me. Had you told me you wanted it before we started, I would have gladly given it to you."

"If that is so," said Mr. Crocodile, "we will have to go back for your heart."

"Yes, hurry," said the monkey, "before your wife gets any worse." Mr. Crocodile turned around and swam back to the rose-apple tree as fast as he could. As soon as they touched the riverbank, Mr. Monkey scampered up the tree, and when he was perched on a high branch out of Mr. Crocodile's reach, he said, "Now you can go back to your wicked wife and tell her that her husband is the greatest fool."

India, along with China, boasts one of the oldest civilizations in the world. The famous Taj Mahal palace has been called one of the seven wonders of the world, while Indian art, science, and literature have had tremendous influence on other cultures. Today, India is one of the most populated countries on earth, creating a huge demand for development assistance. CARE is there—providing school lunches to Indian children, offering credit to poor people who want to start small businesses, providing health services to women and to families, and constructing irrigation systems, roads, community centers, and day-care centers. Every year CARE reaches millions of poor people in India with lifesaving humanitarian assistance.

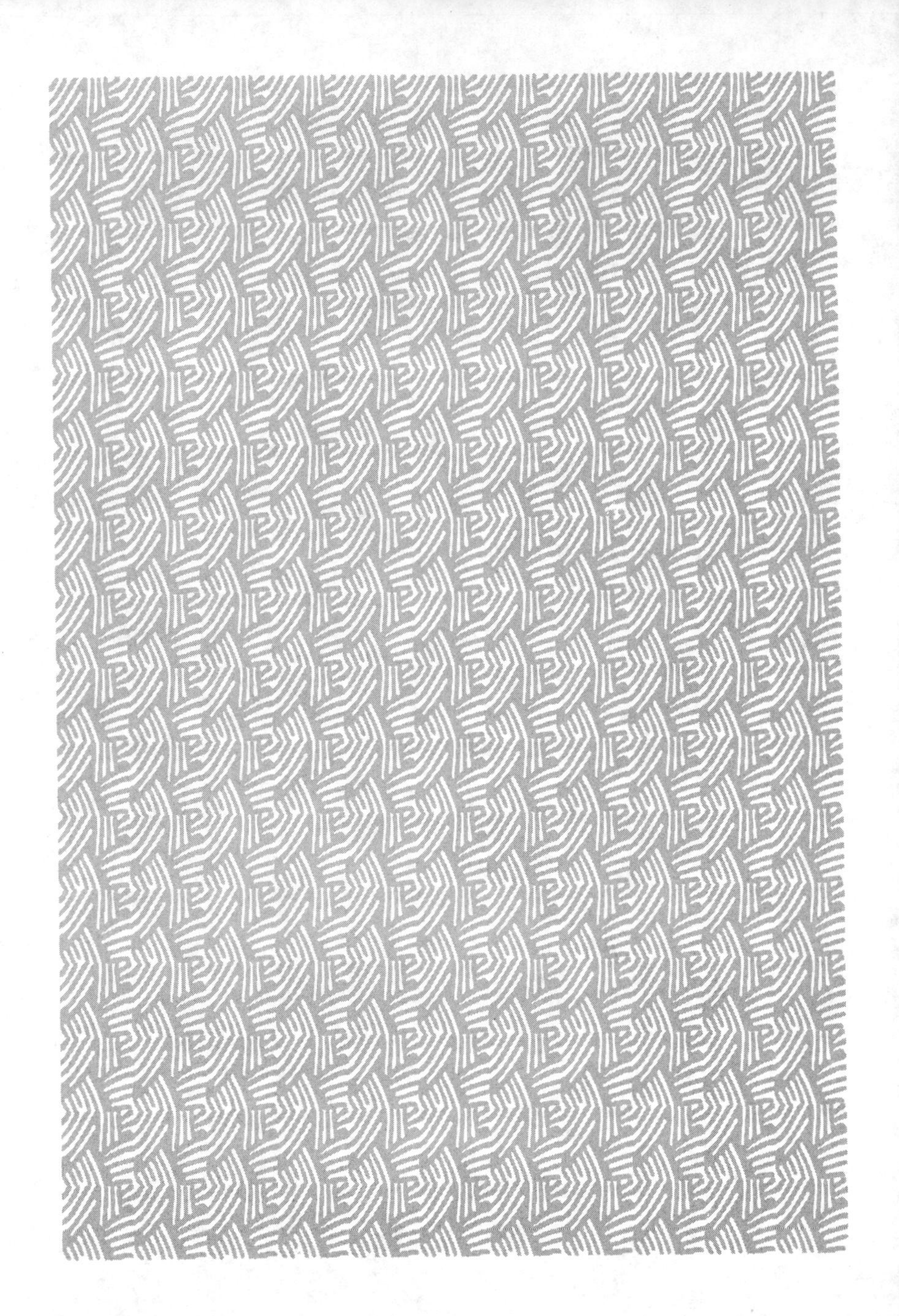

The Swallow's Gift

by Ben Choe

A long, very long time ago, there lived two brothers. The older brother was named Nol-bu and his sibling was named Hoong-bu. Now Nol-bu was a very rich man; he lived very well, but was ill-tempered. Hoong-bu, on the other hand, was very kind and gentle but was very poor. They grew apart and raised their own separate families, Nol-bu in an extravagant mansion as large as a castle, with many servants; Hoong-bu in a tiny, squalid, thatched-roof cottage.

Hoong-bu, a farmer by trade, had seven small children who cried out "We're hungry!" without end. But because his property was so limited, he could not raise enough crops to feed even his own family. So the children were constantly without food.

Now, there were many criminals at this time who were to receive caning strokes on their naked backs for their crimes. Depending on the severity of their crimes, these criminals got from five to fifty strokes. When Hoong-bu needed to feed his family, he would receive a small amount of rice in payment for taking their whippings for them. So he would come home bleeding to feed his hungry children. This is the way he lived; this was how poor he was. But through all this, he was still a gentle and loving soul.

From time to time Hoong-bu would pay a visit to his elder brother, Nol-bu, and tell him that his nieces and nephews were going hungry, and beg for a little rice. From the kitchen where she was cooking, Nol-bu's bad-mannered wife would come out with a rice scooping paddle and strike her brother-in-law in the face with it, saying, "That is the only reason you ever come here, brother, to beg! Get out!" Now, Hoong-bu, being so hungry, could only pick off the grains of rice that the rice paddle had left stuck on his face. Yet he had no enmity toward his brother, Nol-bu, nor toward his brother's wife.

When spring comes to Korea, the swallows migrate from the south and make their nests on the eaves of many homes. Here they raise their hatchlings, and after these grow over the summer season, they all return south. This cycle continues every year.

One day Hoong-bu had finished eating what rice he had managed to glean for the day and was watching a mother swallow drop insects and such into the open, chirping mouths of her helpless baby swallows. Somehow a predatory snake had managed to climb up onto the eaves where the nest had been built and was slithering toward it with the intention of consuming its inhabitants. Hoong-bu, upon seeing this, struck the snake's head and killed it before it harmed the baby birds. But one little baby swallow happened to fall out of the nest and broke its leg on the ground. Hoong-bu took it under his wing and cared for it like one of his own children, feeding it and mending its broken leg.

After the season was over and the swallows had grown up, they were ready to migrate once more to the south. Hoong-bu's baby swallow had completely healed and had grown into a healthy adult. It left with the other swallows of his nest for warmer, more hospitable climates.

The harsh, cold winter gave way once more to springtime and Hoong-bu could hear the swallows returning. "Chirp, chirp," they cried. The swallow whose leg Hoong-bu had tended found his thatched-roof cottage once again and circled around his home. It swooped down and dropped something into Hoong-bu's outstretched hand. It was a pumpkin seed.

So Hoong-bu planted the seed and watered the plant that grew from it. Many vines sprang from the original pumpkin, which grew larger and heavier. And from these vines grew more and more pumpkins, as large and as heavy as the first. When harvest time finally came in October, Hoong-bu and his wife brought out the saws to cut open their pumpkins. But what came out of the pumpkins exceeded even their wildest dream. Money, gold, diamonds, precious jewelry—all this spilled out of each gourd they opened.

Hoong-bu, like his brother, became a very rich and powerful man. He had a castle, larger even than that of Nol-bu's, built where his little cottage once stood. Because of the precious gift of the swallow, Hoong-bu began to live very well, even better than his evil and dishonest brother. Now, Nol-bu heard these rumors about his brother's newfound riches and about how he had elevated himself from the poor farmer he once was to a rich and respected man. He hurried at once to his brother's house and saw that the rumors were not only true, but actually underestimated Hoong-bu's great wealth. "Why, he lives in a more extravagant house, with more richly clothed slaves, than even me!" Nol-bu exclaimed in burning disbelief.

"Why that poor, incapable fool! He who came and took a stroke from my wife's rice paddle! That beggar who used to come to my door on his hands and knees! How is it that he lives like this? Hoong-bu! Who did you steal all this from? If you didn't rob someone, how could you live in such a fine house with as many fine servants? You'd better repent of your crimes at once!" And Nol-bu continued to rain accusations on his brother.

So Hoong-bu, being gentlehearted and a little bit naive, told Nol-bu, "No, brother, it was not that way at all! A swallow was about to be eaten by a snake and fell out of its nest. I fixed its broken leg and sent it on its way. The next spring it came back and gave me this seed that I planted, from which grew pumpkins. Inside these pumpkins were the riches that made me wealthy."

"Ah, is that right?" was Nol-bu's reply.

He went home with the intention of getting his hands on even more treasure than his brother had. As fate would have it, the following spring brought a swallow's nest to the roof of Nol-bu's mansion. But as long as Nol-bu waited, no snake appeared to crawl up and threaten the nest. So the evil brother caught a snake in the fields and deliberately planted it there on his rooftop. At the sight of the predator, the baby swallows began to chirp in alarm and one even fell out of its nest. But its leg was not broken; indeed, it was unharmed. Nol-bu became angry and snapped the baby swallow's leg in half and then mended it.

Well, this swallow also became healed and flew south for the winter and, in the spring, came back to Nol-bu's house with a seed in its beak. Nol-bu grew very excited and planted the large, perfect seed into the ground and proceeded to water and fertilize it. Huge vines and pumpkins grew from the seed, occupying all of Nol-bu's attention and time. His grandiose thoughts of becoming richer and more powerful than Hoong-bu constantly filled his head.

Finally Nol-bu's huge pumpkins were ripe and ready to be opened. So Nol-bu and his wife got out their axes and saws, and together, with great anticipation, they opened up the largest one. To their amazement and disgust, a resounding "Boom!" echoed through their property and torrents of excrement, filth and smoke rushed out of the open gourd, causing Nol-bu and his wife to flee. "This filthy pumpkin was the single rotten one out of all the harvest," a determined Nol-bu told his wife. "We must open all of them."

Upon opening a second, and then a third pumpkin, more and more horrible filth poured out, including snakes, frogs, demons, trolls, and ghosts. Nol-bu, in his voracious greed, opened each of the fat pumpkins, and unleashed a terrible army of evil spirits that tore down his house and left him with absolutely nothing. In time, he faded away and disappeared.

Hoong-bu, meanwhile, prospered and lived happily ever after.

KOREA:

On the easternmost tip of Asia, across the Yellow Sea from China, lies Korea—a country with a history dating back as far as the first century B.C. Today it is divided into two nations, North Korea and South Korea. CARE first started work in Korea after World War II, sending CARE Packages of food to war survivors and later offering seeds and tools so that Koreans could plant crops and grow their own food. Thanks in part to CARE's partnership with South Korea, the country has flourished and CARE was able to close down its operations there in 1979.

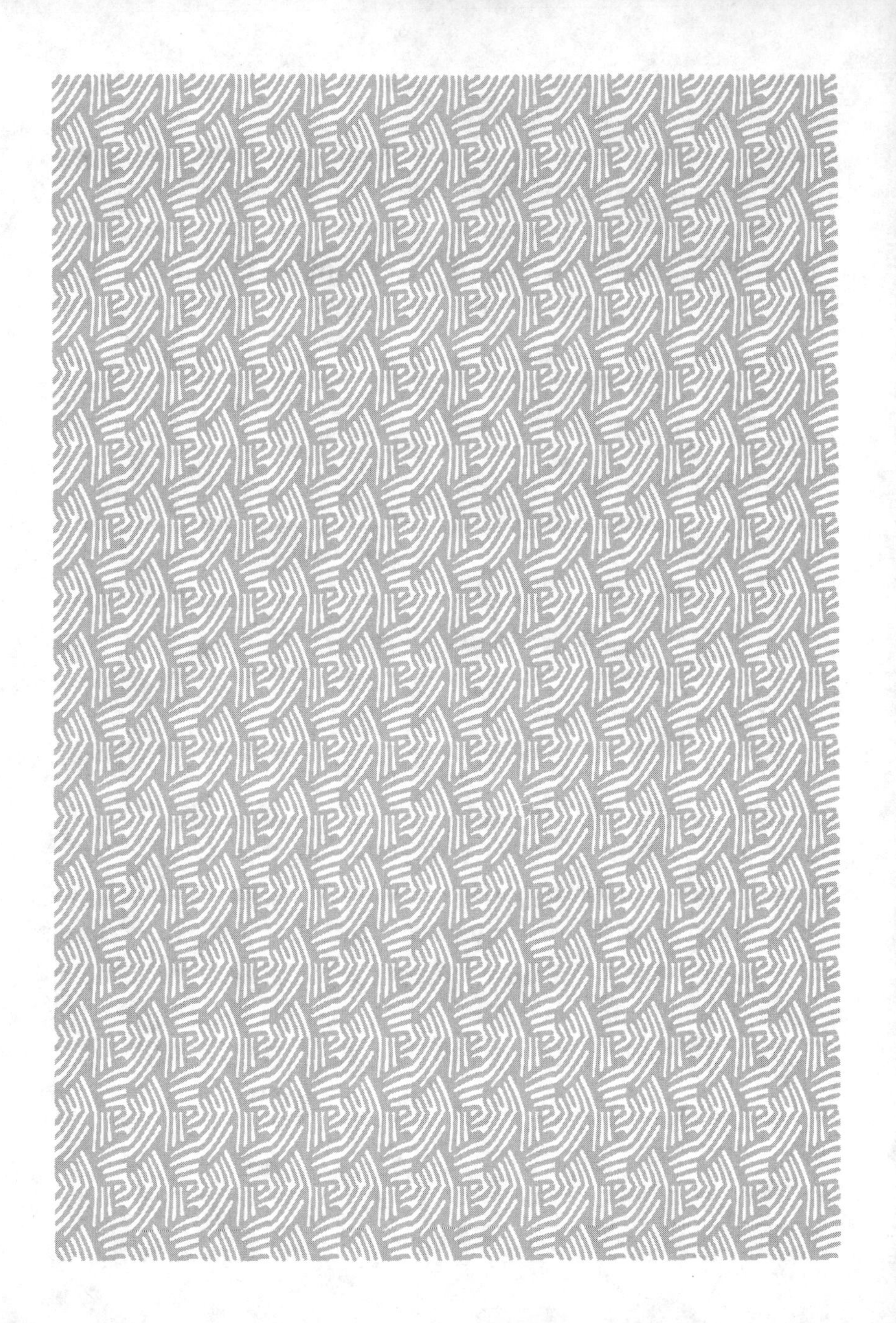

Chhat, The Festival of the Worshipping of the Sun

by Sushila Jha

In ancient times, Nepal was divided into several kingdoms. In the lowlands of Nepal, called the Terai, there were three powerful kings. In the eastern part was King Birat; in the west were the Malla rulers; and the middle region of the Terai, then popularly known as Mithila, was ruled by King Sumanta of the Bidehal dynasty. He was popular and kind. The people of Mithila were very happy and prosperous. But inside the palace there was sadness as the King and Queen had no children.

The Queen knew that if they did not have a child, the Bidehal dynasty would collapse. Then either Birat from the east or the rulers of the Malla dynasty from the west would come and conquer Mithila. She consulted learned scholars and pundits, and even the old men and women of the Kingdom, but all in vain.

The King decided to call a big meeting to see if this problem could be solved. A lot of people gathered together to discuss the matter. Some said a king can make any reforms he likes, but it is not possible to reform his own fate. Others said that if he was fated to have no children, he would not have any. People attending the meeting were also worried because there were rumors from the east and west suggesting that it was better for King Sumanta to choose his heir from either of the neighboring Kingdoms. The people of Mithila did not like this idea at all. They loved their king, and were happy in Mithila and with their way of life. They did not want to be part of the neighboring Kingdoms.

After long discussions, which lasted throughout the day, there were still no answers. The King and Queen became very sad. As the King was about to end the meeting, a hermit with a yellow dress and a turban on his head appeared. The hermit said, "Your Majesty, I know about your trouble. If you will allow me, I would like to give my suggestions to help you and the people of your glorious Kingdom."

The King gave the holy man his permission to offer his advice. The hermit came nearer to the King and said, "Your Majesty, once a sage met me and said that if any person has any kind of mental or physical problems, he should worship the sun in the month of October. According to the lunar calendar, in this month, after the sixth day of full moon, he should worship the setting sun, and on the following day, the rising sun."

The hermit continued, "Once the Abash King was suffering from leprosy. On the advice of the sage he started the worship of the sun. He was cured after a month. The same thing happened with a merchant in Paichhove. He also was cured after worshiping the sun."

Everybody in the meeting was listening and paying great attention to these stories. The hermit said that the worshipping of the sun was a difficult task. You must fast for three days starting from the fifth day of the full moon, when the worship begins. On the third day you are allowed to eat only in the evenings. The food should be a plain pudding cooked with roasted sugar. It must

not contain any salt or vegetables. On the sixth day of the full moon, you should not take even a drop of water. In the evening, the person fasting should go to a public pond to take a bath. There, he should offer homemade sweets, sugarcane, fruits and green vegetables to the setting sun. Next morning, the same offerings should be made to the rising sun. On hearing these directions from the hermit, the King and Queen said that they would perform this worship from that year. They thanked the holy man for his advice.

When the month of October came, the King and Queen fasted and worshiped the sun. After a month, good news spread throughout the whole kingdom about the Queen's pregnancy. After nine months the Queen gave birth to a healthy son. There were celebrations for a week. Poor people were given delicious food and clothes. Ever since that time the Chhat festival has been celebrated widely in the Terai.

High in the majestic mountain range of the Himalayas lies the Asian country of Nepal. Known as much for its mythical capital city, Katmandu, as for its soaring Mount Everest—the highest mountain in the world—Nepal is a beautiful but poor country. CARE helps poor Nepalese to improve their lives through health and nutrition programs. CARE also teaches farmers how to grow more and better food on the rugged Nepalese hills.

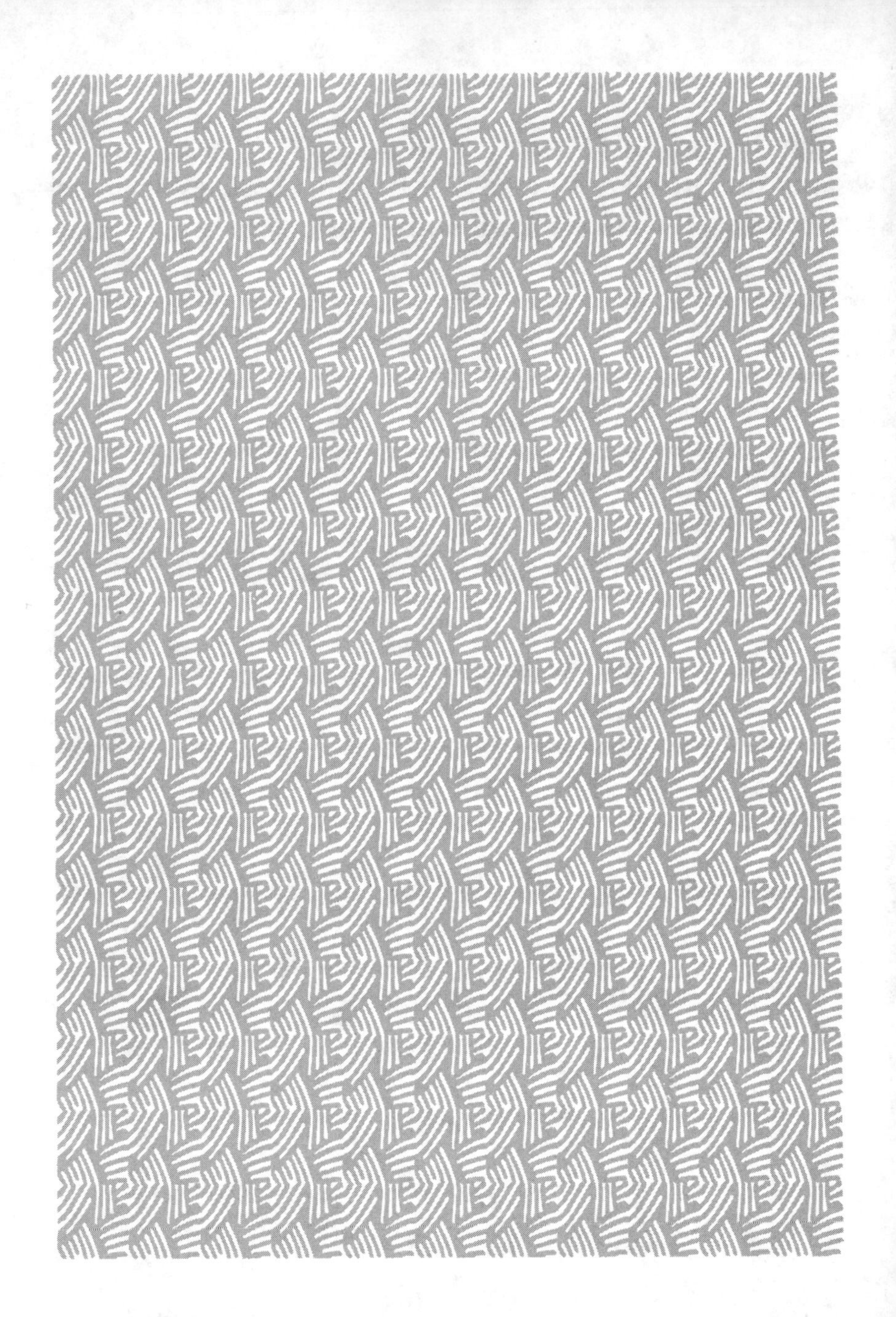

The Magical Song of the Adarna

by Luisito R. Baclagon

A LONG, long time ago, a king named Fernando ruled the kingdom of Berbania. The king ruled well and wisely: that is why the kingdom was very peaceful and prosperous for so many years.

The King had three sons who were all worthy heirs to the royal throne. The eldest, Don Pedro, was brave and strong. Don Diego, the second, was an excellent hunter. Don Juan, the youngest, was kind and helpful. Among the three, it was Don Juan who was loved by all the people in the Kingdom.

One day King Fernando suddenly fell ill. And what a strange and serious illness it was! Not even the best doctors in the Kingdom could make him well. The three Princes could only watch helplessly as the doctors tried cure upon cure on the hopeless King. Because everyone loved the King, the whole Kingdom wept and prayed for him.

Then an old sage came to the palace to see the ailing King. "Well," said Don Pedro, "can you make him well?"

"There's only one thing that can cure His Majesty," the sage said.

"Then go and get it!" Don Diego commanded.

"We will do everything to save our father," Don Juan said, distraught.

"The song of the Adarna!" replied the sage. "Its magical song will make the King well."

"What is an Adarna?" asked Don Pedro.

"Adarna is a bird of wonder," said the sage.

"Where can we buy such a bird?" asked Don Pedro.

"My dear highness," explained the sage, "no amount of money can buy the Adarna. It is an enchanted and elusive bird. One must persevere to catch it."

"Where can I find it?" asked Don Diego, because he was an excellent hunter.

"The Adarna lives in the tree of Piedras Platas, on the high peak of Mount Tabor."

"Then I will leave at once to look for it," declared Don Pedro, because he was the eldest of the King's three sons.

"Be prepared, Your Highness," warned the old man, "for the journey will be long and difficult."

"My courage has not yet failed me," said Don Pedro.

And so Don Pedro set out on his journey. He crossed many rivers and forests. But he could not find Mount Tabor. He asked everyone he met about the mountain and the Adarna, but no one knew where or what it was. Suddenly a wretched old man appeared on the way. The old man's long gray hair was so dirty that it was caked with mud. His skin, full of wrinkles, warts, and freckles, also abounded in sores and rashes. He wore tattered sackcloth smeared with all sort of dirt and dust. "Young man, please help me," the old man begged Don Pedro. "I am very hungry and thirsty. A little food and water are all I need."

"Hey! Do not come near me, old man," Don Pedro exclaimed. "I am a prince and it is not proper for a dirty beggar like you to come near me."

"Please, young man, only a little food and water. Please help me...."

"I need all my food and water to last for my journey. And even if I had more, I would not think of giving them to you. So go away, go away!"

The old man was about to turn away when Don Pedro said, "Wait, old man! Do you know where Mount Tabor is?"

The old man pointed to the tall blue mountain that was lying in the east. "That is Mount Tabor," he said. "Now may I have a few drops of water?"

"As I told you, old man," replied Don Pedro, "the water I have is just enough for me." Then he headed off quickly for Mount Tabor.

It was already evening when Don Pedro reached the top of Mount Tabor. And there it was: the amazing tree! Its leaves were silk with gold linings, while its silvery trunk and branches were studded with sparkling diamonds and sapphires. "This must be the tree of Piedras Platas," Don Pedro said as he marveled at the tree. Tired but excited, he sat beside a white stone and waited for the enchanted bird to arrive. Moments later he heard a fluttering of wings on top of the Piedras Platas. And as he looked up he saw the most beautiful thing he has ever seen in his whole life. "The Adarna bird! The Adarna bird!" The Adarna was like a queen in full regalia. It had horns that looked like a diamond-studded crown. Its feathers were strong, thick, and shiny, while its full and very long tail hung like an embroidered wedding train on a royal bridal gown.

Then the Adarna began to sing. It was the sweetest and most melodious song that Don Pedro had ever heard. And then the Adarna's feathers changed colors, seven times, into ruby red, sunset orange, peach yellow, emerald green, satin blue, velvet violet, and deep indigo. And while this was going on, Don Pedro slowly dropped off to sleep. Nothing can keep someone from sleeping when the enchanted bird sings.

As soon as it finished its last song, the Adarna defecated and proceeded to go to sleep. But alas! The bird's droppings fell on the sleeping Don Pedro. And Don Pedro turned into a huge white stone!

When Don Diego followed his brother's quest, he met the same fate. He suffered many difficulties along the way. He met the wretched old man and ignored his pleadings. And when he found the Adarna in Piedras Platas, he, too, fell asleep while marveling at the sight and listening, enchanted, to the songs of the magical bird. Afterward, Don Diego, too, was turned into a stone.

Back in the palace, Don Juan was restless. "My father is getting weaker and weaker. And there is no word about my brothers. I must go find them myself," he decided.

Like his brothers, Don Juan met the wretched old man, who pleaded, "Water, please, water..."

The young Prince led the old man into the shade of a tree. There, he let the old man drink from his flask. He also laid out some bread for the old man to eat.

"But you, too, have to eat," said the old man to Don Juan.

"Don't worry," Don Juan said comfortingly. "I am young and strong. You need food and water more than I do."

Suddenly, with those words, the old man's appearance changed. Gone were the dirty clothes and his sores, which had so disgusted Don Pedro and Don Diego. "You are the old sage who told us to look for the Adarna bird!" Juan exclaimed.

"Yes, Your Highness," the sage explained. "I stood on this path to test you and your brothers. Because you have the kindest heart of all, I will help you catch the Adarna bird." Then, showing Don Juan a dagger, a lemon fruit, and a vial of magical water, he said, "Take these. When the Adarna starts to sing, cut your arms slightly with the dagger, then rub the lemon juice on your wounds. It will keep you awake."

"What will I do with the water?" asked Don Juan.

"Sprinkle it on the big white stones under the tree of Piedras Platas," the sage answered.

"Stones?" asked Don Juan.

"The stones were formerly humans until the droppings of the Adarna fell on them," explained the sage. Then he told the Prince where the mysterious mountain was located and what to expect when he got there.

At last, Don Juan reached Mount Tabor. Like his brothers, he marveled at the sight of the place. A few moments later the Adarna flew in. Yes, Don Juan thought, he is right, the Adarna is a most beautiful bird! Then the bird sat on one of the tree's big branches. And Don Juan breathlessly hid behind a big white stone to catch the bird.

Again, the Adarna began to sing. As it sang its glossy plumage started to change colors seven times. The sweetness of the song made Don Juan's eyes grow heavy. But he remembered the words of the old sage. Slightly cutting his arms, he squeezed lemon juice on the wound. He felt a sharp, stinging pain. And just as the sage said, the unbearable pain kept him wide-awake.

Then the Adarna closed its eyes. As Don Juan slowly set himself to catch it, he remembered the words of the old man: "The Adarna excretes before it sleeps." And just as the bird performed its sleeping ritual, Don Juan was able to move aside and avoid the bird's droppings, which turned humans into stones. Then he climbed up the tree and succeeded in catching the enchanted bird.

As Don Juan climbed down he noticed the big white stones under the Piedras Platas. And just as the old man had advised him, he sprinkled the magic water on the stones. And lo and behold! The stones turned back into humans. Don Juan was overjoyed to see his brothers Don Pedro and Don Diego standing among them.

And so the three brothers happily journeyed home. Don Juan cradled the Adarna in his arms. And just as soon as the King heard the Adarna's magical song, he became strong, healthy and happy again. The whole Kingdom rejoiced and celebrated when they heard the good news.

And the moral of the story? Success is nearest to the one with the kindliest heart.

The Philippines:

The Philippines are a collection of lush, tropical islands lying between the South China Sea and the Philippine Sea. Filipinos—as the island's people call themselves—have a diverse culture inherited from centuries of visitors from China, Spain, and nearby Asian countries. CARE provides school lunches to poor children in the Philippines. CARE also offers Philippine families health care, educational programs, agricultural and environmental improvement and relief aid.

European Stories

The Boy of Good Fortune and the Devil's Golden Hairs

by Susan Krauss

Once upon a time, there lived a man and woman of poor means who gave birth to a son, a special boy for whom a wise old man of the village prophesied marriage to the King's daughter in his fourteenth year. The poor woman rejoiced at such a prediction, a chance for her son to achieve greatness far beyond her own dreams.

Not long after the boy was born, the King was traveling through the land, visiting his subjects. He was a selfish king with an evil heart, who traveled from village to village scouting for news from each corner of his Kingdom that he might use to his advantage.

When he came to this particular village, the King asked of the villagers what news they might bestow upon him since his last visit. One of the townspeople told the King that a child had been born for whom a sage had prophesied good fortune, and that in his fourteenth year he would have the King's daughter for a wife.

The King flew into a rage over the prophecy and returned to his castle to brood over this grave event. He paced the great hall over and over until he devised a plan, his most devious ever, he concluded with an evil grin. That very next day the King disguised himself as a rich merchant and went to visit the child's parents. Pretending to be kind to them, the King said, "You are poor yet good people, and I would like to help you. Let me take your child to raise in my own household. Since I am a well-to-do man, I can provide more than amply for the child and he will live a life of luxurious means without want."

They considered this proposition; after all, it was prophesied that their son would come into great fortune, and perhaps this merchant was here to realize the prophecy. However, this was not what they were expecting at all—to relinquish their baby to a stranger. So at first they refused. But the King was not to be deterred and offered them a large amount of gold for the child. The father considered this and suggested, "He is a child of good fortune, and everything must turn out well for him." So at last they consented, and gave the King the child.

The King put the little baby in a box and left the village. He rode until he came to a deep river into which he cast the box and thought with deep satisfaction, "I have freed my daughter from her undesired suitor." And he rode away home, content that his task had been so masterfully and expeditiously completed.

The box tossed and tumbled in the river, bobbing up and down, but did not sink. Remaining tight and dry, it floated along downriver like a small boat. After a time it drifted to a mill near the King's chief city and came to rest against the dam of the mill. The miller's boy saw the strange box and quickly pulled it out, thinking he had found a great treasure. He opened the box, and much to his surprise there lay within a pretty baby boy, awake and crying. He brought the baby to the miller and his wife, who had no children of their own. Upon seeing the baby, they rejoiced and said, "God has given him to us." They

took great care of the foundling, and he grew up enjoying all the goodness they could offer.

Many years passed. One day the King was again on his tour of visits to the villages in his Kingdom and was caught in a great storm that raged so fiercely that he sought shelter. The King saw the mill and knocked upon its door. The miller and his wife offered their home to him for as long as he might wish to take refuge from the storm. The King spoke with a tall youth whose good manners pleased him and asked casually if the boy was their son.

"No," they answered, "he's a foundling. Fourteen years ago he floated down to the mill dam in a box, and the mill boy pulled him out of the water."

The King was astounded—this youth was none other than the child of good fortune whom he had cast into the water. The King smiled in knowledge that his own good fortune had taken him to this mill this day so that he might truly complete the task he had set out to finish fourteen years before. The King said to the miller and his wife: "My good people, I need this youth to take a letter to the Queen. I will give him two gold pieces as a reward."

Thankful for the King's gracious and most generous offer, the miller answered, "Just as you say, O King," and told the youth to prepare for his trip. Then the

King wrote a letter to the Queen, which read, *My Queen, as soon as the boy arrives with this letter, let him be killed and buried, and all must be done before I return.* He folded and sealed the letter and handed it to the boy with explicit instructions that it not be opened, lest he incur the Queen's wrath and suffer great punishment.

The boy set out with the letter, but as evening was falling he lost his way in the great forest that separated the mill from the King's castle. He continued to wander aimlessly until in the far reaches of the darkness he saw a small light. As he approached this light he saw that it came from a farmhouse. Upon arriving, he met an old woman sitting by the fire, alone. She started up in fright, and asked the boy, "My young lad, from where do you come alone and at this late hour, and whither are you going?"

"I come from the village near the river," the boy replied. "I have been sent by the King to bring his queen this message." He held up the letter to her and then lowered his head in shame. "Alas, I have lost my way in the forest and am remiss at fulfilling my duties this day. May I stay until the morrow?" he asked.

"You poor boy," said the old woman, "this home that you have found is one of thieves, and when they return, they will surely kill you if you remain here."

"I am too tired to be afraid," the boy said. "I am so tired that I cannot go any farther." Then he yawned and stretched himself on a bench and fell fast asleep.

Soon the robbers came home and demanded of the old woman to explain the presence of the strange boy who lay upon their bench. "Ah," said the old woman, "he is but an innocent young lad who has gotten lost in the forest, and out of pity I let him stay and spend the night. He has with him a letter for the Queen."

The robbers delighted at this—here was something of value that they might steal from this young boy. They removed the letter from his outstretched hands, opened it, and read the contents. In it was written that the boy should be put to death upon his arrival. Even for robbers this seemed cruel; what could this little boy have done to be sent to deliver his own death decree to the nasty Queen for whom they held only resentment and contempt?

The hard-hearted robbers took pity on the boy and their leader tore up the letter, replacing it with another written in his own hand that read, *As soon as this boy arrives, he should be married at once to the King's daughter*. They drank tankards of ale and laughed with great mirth at the deception they were to put over on the King and Queen. They let the boy sleep quietly through the night, and the next morning they gave him the letter and sent him on his way with directions to the castle.

When he reached the Queen, he presented the letter, which she opened and read. She then proceeded to comply with its instructions and prepared a wonderful wedding celebration. Thus the King's daughter was married to the child of good fortune at the castle.

Many weeks later the King returned to his palace and nearly fell off his horse when he heard the news of his daughter's wedding. His temper flared when he realized that the prophecy had been fulfilled: the child of good fortune had indeed married his daughter. The King was very angry and had the page who delivered the news sent to the dungeon. He was absolutely perplexed and sought out his queen, to whom he asked, "How could this have come to pass? Did you not receive my message from the boy?"

The Queen nodded that she had received his letter and handed it to him. The King read the letter and saw quite well that it was not the one he himself had penned. He called for the youth and asked him what had become of the letter he had given him and if he did not indeed remember the King's warning about reading the letter. The boy replied innocently, "I know not of anything. I can only surmise that it must have been changed in the night I spent in the forest."

The King burned with rage over his defeat. Not being a man used to losing any contest or battle, he quickly thought and regained his composure, thinking again in his most devious manner of what evil he could contrive to rid himself of this youth once and for all without his daughter's knowledge of his intent.

The King spoke unto the boy: "Whosoever marries my daughter must first be able to complete one task. You must go to Hell and get three golden hairs from the head of the Devil. Once you have brought me these three precious hairs, you will then be able to keep my daughter. Otherwise, you shall not be considered worthy of my daughter." The King had hoped this daunting task would discourage the boy, and he would rid himself of him forever.

But the child of good fortune boldly accepted his challenge. "I will go find the devil and fetch the golden hairs." Whereupon he took leave of the King and Queen and began his journey to find Hell.

The boy took a road that eventually led him to a large town. There, he met a watchman by the gates who asked him what his trade was and what he knew.

"There is nothing that I do not know," answered the child of good fortune.

"Then perhaps you can help us with this puzzling problem that has occurred," said the watchman. "Our

market fountain, which once flowed with wine, has become dry, and no longer gives even water. Perhaps you can tell us why it has stopped working."

"That I can answer," replied the youth, "only it must wait until I return." The boy continued his journey and came to another town. There he met another gatekeeper who asked him what was his trade and what he knew.

"There is nothing that I do not know," the boy answered again.

"Then, please help us solve this problem," asked the second gatekeeper. "There is a tree in our town which once bore beautiful golden apples. Now it is fruitless and does not even put forth leaves. Can you tell us why this has happened?"

"That I can answer," replied the youth, "only it must wait until I return." The boy continued on and came to a wide river that he sought to cross. He met a ferryman who asked him what his trade was and what he knew. "There is nothing that I do not know," he answered a third time.

"Then please help me with this problem," said the ferryman. "I am always rowing backward and forward. How can I be set free and still run my ferry?"

"That I can answer," replied the boy, "only it must wait until I return." When he had crossed the river, the boy found the entrance to Hell. It was dark and hot as he entered and he saw that the Devil was not at home. Instead, he found an elderly woman sitting in a large armchair.

She looked up at the youth and asked in a cackling voice, "Who are you, my young lad?"

"I have come in search of three of the Devil's golden hairs," answered the boy as he shivered a bit, "so that I will be able to please the King and keep my wife."

"That is a difficult thing to ask for," warned the old woman. "If the Devil comes home and finds you here, he will surely do away with you. But as I pity you, I will see if I cannot help you."

The old woman chanted a spell and the youth turned into a mouse. Beckoning him to her, she said, "Come here and hide in the pockets of my apron, where you will be safe."

The boy who was now a little brown furry mouse climbed into her apron pockets, but before he became quiet, he spoke to the old woman, "There are three questions that I must have answered: Why a fountain that once flowed with wine and water has become dry; why a tree which once bore beautiful golden apples does not even put forth leaves, and why a ferryman must always be going backward and forward, and is never set free?"

"Indeed, these are difficult questions; however, they are not at all unanswerable. Just be quiet and I will get the

Devil to help us while I pluck his golden hairs," said the old woman.

When evening came, the Devil returned home and sat down to eat his supper. When he had eaten and drunk until he was tired, he laid his head on the old woman's lap and fell into a deep sleep.

The old woman then took hold of a golden strand of hair and, with a quick flick of her wrist, plucked it out and put it in her apron pocket. "Old woman," cried the Devil, "what are you doing?"

"I have had a bad dream, and out of fright I seized hold of your hair," she replied while pretending to be still somewhat sleepy.

"What was your bad dream, old woman?" asked the Devil.

"In my dream, there was a beautiful fountain that always had the most delicious wine flowing out from its spout. Then one day it dried up and no wine, not even water, would flow out of it. Why was this so?" asked the old woman.

"Old woman, that is an easy one to answer. Why, surely, everyone, if they were as smart as I, would have looked to find a toad sitting under a stone in the well. Killing the toad would have renewed the fountain, which would then have surely poured forth the delicious wine as it did before," said the Devil.

Again the Devil went back to a deep sleep, whereupon the old woman pulled out the second hair. "Old woman! Are you mad!" the Devil cried out.

"Do not be angry with me," said she. "I have had another bad dream."

"What have you dreamed this time?" he asked with a little less patience.

"I dreamed that in a certain kingdom there stood an apple tree which had once borne beautiful golden apples, but now would not even bear leaves. What, think you, was the reason?"

"Oh! Surely, the answer is obvious," replied the Devil. "A mouse was gnawing at the root. All that had to be done was to kill the mouse, upon which the tree would have again bore golden apples, unless the root has been gnawed too much. In that case, the tree would wither altogether. Now, old woman, enough of your dreams and let me go back to sleep!"

The old woman spoke softly to the Devil once more until he fell asleep and snored. Then she took hold of the third golden hair and pulled it out. The Devil jumped up and roared out in anger once again. To calm him down, the old woman looked at him and tried to justify herself. "I am sorry, but I cannot seem to stop having bad dreams."

"Alas, old woman, what was the dream this time then?" The Devil sighed loudly as he spoke.

"I dreamed of a ferryman who complained that he must always ferry from one side to the other and was never released. What was the cause of it, I wonder but cannot devise?" asked the old woman.

"Ah! The poor fool," the Devil remarked. "If anyone wanted to go across, the ferryman would have had to put the oar in his hand while the other man ferried the launch. Only then would he be free."

As the old woman had plucked out the three golden hairs, and the three questions were answered, she let the old Devil alone, and he slept until daybreak.

When the Devil left the house, the old woman took the little mouse out of her apron pocket and turned the child of good fortune back into his human form again. "Now, here are your three golden hairs. And you heard the Devil's answers to your three questions?" asked she. The young boy nodded yes. "Now quickly, be off as fast as you can from this inferno, and be careful not to run into the Devil!" warned the old woman.

Offering the old woman, who had indeed done him a great service, profuse thanks, the boy began his journey home.

On his way back, he came to the ferryman to whom he had originally promised an answer. "Take me across the river first," said the child of good fortune," and then I will tell you how you can be set free." And when he had reached the opposite shore, he gave the ferryman the Devil's advice: "Next time anyone takes your ferry, just put the oar in his hand."

He continued on and returned to the town where he had met the second watchman. "I have the answer to your question about your town's fruitless tree," the boy announced. "Kill the mouse which is gnawing at its root. Once that it is done, the tree will again bear beautiful golden apples." The watchman thanked him profusely and gave him a reward of two bags of gold.

Finally, he reached his last stop, the town whose well had gone dry. He told the watchman, "There is a toad blocking the well beneath the fountain. Find and kill it, and the well will again spring forth with your delicious wine." The watchman thanked him profusely and also gave him two bags of gold.

At last, the boy returned home to his wife, who was very happy to see him. The boy then presented the King with the Devil's three golden hairs. When the King saw the four bags laden with gold he was quite content, and said: "Now all the conditions are fulfilled, and you can keep my daughter. But tell me, dear son-in-law, where did all that gold come from? This is tremendous wealth!"

"I was rowed across a river," answered the boy, "and got it there; it lies on the shore instead of sand."

"Can I, too, fetch some of it?" said the King eagerly, with eyes of intense greed.

"As much as you like," answered the youth. "There is a ferryman on the river; let him ferry you over, and you can fill your sacks on the other side."

The greedy King set out all in haste, and when he came to the river, he beckoned to the ferryman to put him across. The ferryman came and bade him get in, and when they got to the other shore, he put the oar in his hand and sprang out.

And from this time forth the King had to ferry back and forth, and was never released, as punishment for his sins. Perhaps he is ferrying still, if no one has taken the oar from him.

Germany:

At the end of World War II, much of Germany lay in ruins. The German people, who had lost the war against the Western Allies, were hungry and destitute. Then a miracle happened: a CARE Package came. These plain brown boxes of food, medicine, and other relief supplies were America's way of reaching out to needy German war survivors and other Europeans in desperate straits. The CARE Packages—and the generosity they symbolized—became so famous that today they are synonymous with

any gift between friends. Germany, meanwhile, recovered through the help of CARE and other organizations and today has its own CARE office, through which it offers help to poor countries in the developing world.

POLAND

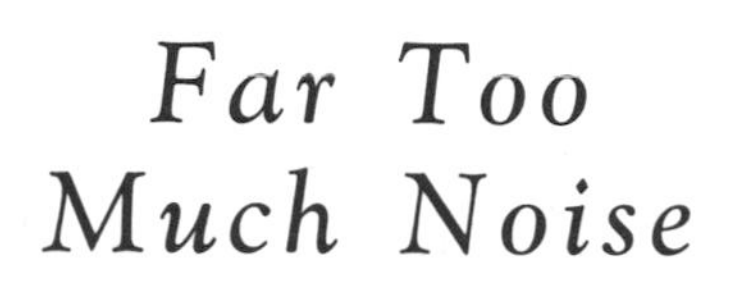

Far Too Much Noise

adapted by Sandy Pomerantz

In a village in Prussia in
days long gone by,
Mendel the farmer went
to his learned rabbi.

"Rabbi, O Rabbi, my
world's full of strife,
My relatives moved in with
me and my wife.

My daughter, her husband, and their two
bouncy boys.
My house is too crowded! There's far too much
noise!"

The rabbi was having some tea and some
challah,
He looked in the Talmud, consulted Kabbala.
He took off his spectacles; he scratched at
his head;
He looked up at Mendel and here's what
he said:

"Mendel, dear Mendel, here's what you must do.
Take the dog from the yard and move it in, too.
You're asking me once; I'm telling you twice.
Move the dog to the house. That is my advice!"

Mendel went home; this wasn't too hard.
He brought the old dog to the house from
the yard.
The dog barked a lot and got in the way.
Mendel went back to the rabbi next day.

"Rabbi, O Rabbi, I did just what you said,
And now I'm afraid I'll go out of my head.

The dog barks...bow-wow.
There's my daughter, her husband, and their
two bouncy boys.
My house is too crowded! There's far too
much noise!"

"Mendel, dear Mendel, here's what you
must do.
Take the hens from their nests and move
them in, too.
You're asking me once; I'm telling you twice.
Move the hens to the house. That is my
advice!"

Though he doubted the sense of his rabbi's
request,
Mendel brought all the hens to the house from
their nests.
The hens clucked and squawked, laid their eggs
everywhere.
Next day at the rabbi's house, Mendel was
there.

"Rabbi, O Rabbi, I know you are kind;
But I'm sure that I'm going right out of my mind.
The hens squawk . . . squawk-squawk.

The dog barks . . . bow-wow.
My daughter, her husband, and their two
bouncy boys.
My house is too crowded! There's far too much
noise!"

"Mendel, dear Mendel, here's what you must
do.
Take the geese from their pen and move them
in, too.
You're asking me once; I'm telling you twice.
Move the geese to the house. That is my
advice!"

Mendel went home, shook his head once again;
But he brought all the geese to the house from
their pen.
The geese honked all day and nibbled on toes.
Next day back went Mendel to tell of his woes.

"Rabbi, O Rabbi, I don't understand!
Things back at my house have got quite out of
hand.
The geese honk . . . honk-honk.
The hens squawk . . . squawk-squawk.
The dog barks . . . bow-wow.

My daughter, her husband, and their two
bouncy boys.
My house is too crowded! There's far too much
noise!"

"Mendel, dear Mendel, here's what you
must do.
Take the goat from the shed and move it in, too.
You're asking me once; I'm telling you twice.
Move the goat to the house. That is my advice!"

Though he thought the rabbi might be out of
his head,
Mendel moved in the goat to the house from
the shed.
The goat smelled quite strong and ate all food
in sight.
Next day Mendel returned to tell of his plight.

"Rabbi, *oy vay,* Rabbi, I don't know what to do!
How would you feel if my animals all moved in
with you?
The goat bleats . . . maa-maa.
The geese honk . . . honk-honk.
The hens squawk . . . squawk-squawk.
The dog barks . . . bow-wow.

My daughter, her husband, and their two
bouncy boys.
My house is too crowded! There's far too
much noise!"

"Mendel, dear Mendel, here's what you must
do.
Take the cows from the barn and move them
in, too.
You're asking me once; I'm telling you twice.
Move the cows to the house. That's your rabbi's
advice!"

Though Mendel was sure it would only do harm,
He moved the two cows to the house from the
barn.
They mooed constantly and knocked everything
down.
So the next day poor Mendel went back into
town.

"Rabbi, *oy vay's mere,* Rabbi, my wife's talking
divorce!
I'm afraid what will be if I stay on this course.
The cows moo . . . moo-moo.
The goats bleats . . . maa-maa.

The geese honk . . . honk-honk.
The hens squawk . . . squawk-squawk.
The dog barks . . . bow-wow.
There's my daughter, her husband, and their two bouncy boys.
My house is too crowded! There's far too much noise!"

"Mendel, my dear Mendel, what I say won't take long.
Now put all of your animals back where they belong!
Put them back once, and clean your house twice;
And I think you will thank me for my good advice!"

So Mendel ran home just as fast as he could.
And he emptied his house, and he cleaned it up good.
There was plenty of room, much to his great surprise;
And the place was so quiet. Mendel's rabbi was wise.

Mendel the farmer had a pretty good life,

Took care of his animals, still lived with his
wife,
Their daughter, her husband, and their two
bouncy boys.
Now his house was all right.
There was just enough noise.

Devastated by war in the 1940s, Polish people were overjoyed by the delivery of millions of packages of food, clothing, medicine, and other relief supplies from America. These CARE Packages delivered by the relief group CARE helped the Poles rebuild their country. Though CARE no longer works extensively in Poland, it does offer health care seminars to Polish doctors.

The Wise Girl

by Sudha Rajagopolan

There once were two brothers who lived in a little village: a poor one who had a poorly fed mare, and a rich one who had a grand horse-drawn cart. One day they both set off to a nearby village to visit some of their relatives. It was nighttime and so they decided to rest under a tree, and while they were asleep, the mare gave birth to a beautiful little colt.

In the morning the rich brother awoke to see the colt cramped up underneath his cart. He woke his poor brother and said to him: "Behold, my cart has given birth to a little colt."

The poor brother didn't believe him and said, "This is impossible, it must have been my mare—carts do not give birth to little horses."

The rich brother exclaimed, "No, it is lying under my cart. If it was your mare, then it would be near your mare!"

The two brothers fought over the colt for more than an hour and finally the poor one suggested that they must go to the Czar to resolve the dispute. The Czar was very wise and the other brother agreed to abide by his decision.

Later that day, they reached the Czar, who listened to both of their stories at length. Finally the Czar suggested: "I will give you four riddles to answer and you must come back to me in three days with the answers to these riddles. The one who answers all of them properly will have ownership of the fine colt."

The Czar continued: "The first riddle is 'What in the world is the most powerful and strongest thing?' The second riddle is 'What is the softest of all things in

the world?' The third riddle is 'What is the sweetest of everything in the world?' And the fourth and final riddle is 'What is the most endowed thing in the world?' If neither of you finds the answers to all four questions, the colt shall be mine." He hadn't gotten to be Czar for nothing. The two brothers agreed.

They both set off in search of the answers without a clue of how to solve the riddles. The rich brother met an old lady on the street and the old lady asked, "Why do you look so crestfallen, young man? What is wrong?"

And he told her his problem. "My cart gave birth to a colt and now I have to prove it to the Czar. And before I do that, I have to answer four riddles."

The old lady asked, "What are they?"

He answered, "The Czar wants to know what is the most powerful and strongest thing in the world?"

The old lady said, "Well, that's easy. I have this little mare and she's faster than anything on earth. She is so swift and powerful that she can chase little rabbits and overtake one in no time at all."

The brother's face brightened and he said, "Oh, that is wonderful. Would you have the answers to my other riddles?"

She responded confidently, "Yes."

The brother asked, "What is the softest thing in the world?"

She answered without hesitation. “That’s easy, there is nothing softer than a little feather bed.”

And quickly he asked the third riddle: “What is the sweetest thing in the world?”

The old lady smiled and said: “My grandson Ivan.”

The brother asked the fourth and final riddle: “What is the most endowed thing?”

She answered with ease: “My pig. I took it into my custody last year and I have been feeding it, and now it can’t even stand on its own two feet.”

The rich brother hugged and thanked her jubilantly. “Oh, my wonderful old woman, you have appeased me and you have given me all these words of wisdom that I will take to the Czar as answers to his four questions.” The rich brother set off to see the Czar.

Meanwhile the poor brother, sad and distraught, saw his little daughter Allonushea, who was just seven years old. She asked, “What is it, Father, why are you looking so crestfallen?”

He answered, “I have to answer these four riddles to prove that my mare gave birth to a little colt.”

Allonushea asked innocently, “What are the riddles?”

He responded, “What is the most powerful and strongest thing in the world?”

She looked up in the sky and then back at her father, answering, “The wind.”

The poor brother looked up as if awakening from sleep and asked the second riddle: "What is the sweetest thing in the world?"

And she answered, "There is nothing sweeter than a dream."

Alive with hope, he asked, "What do you think is the softest thing in the world?"

And she said, "There is nothing softer than your hand. That is why you put it under your head when you sleep."

Finally, he asked of her, "My little one, what is the most endowed thing in the world?"

She answered, "The earth, because it doesn't grow, but it is always feeding and it is always giving us life."

He kissed her forehead and went off to see the Czar. The rich brother and the poor brother met at the Czar's court and the Czar put the riddles to them again. They gave him their answers.

The Czar first turned to the poor brother and said, "Those are interesting answers. Who taught you those or are those your own words of wisdom?"

The poor brother answered, "I have a seven-year-old daughter who told me these answers."

The Czar said, "Well, if she is so wise, then, I have another problem for her." He handed the poor brother a single thread and bade him: "Take this small silken thread give it to her and tell her that I want a beautifully embroidered towel spun out of this one silken thread by tomorrow morning."

Once again, the poor man went back home looking crestfallen, and once again Allonushea asked, "What is it, Father, what is wrong?"

He answered, "You have to make a beautifully embroidered towel by tomorrow morning with this one silken thread."

She answered gaily and to her father's surprise, "That is no problem, I can deal with this."

Allonushea went to a tree and picked a twig off a branch and she gave it to him. She said, "You go to the Czar tomorrow and tell him to build me a loom out of this in one day. Tell him to find a craftsman who can make a loom out of this one twig and with that loom I shall weave his towel."

So he went back to the Czar the next day and told him what his daughter had said. The Czar laughed and replied, "If she is so wise, give her these one hundred fifty eggs and tell her I want one hundred fifty chickens by tomorrow."

So the poor brother again went back to his daughter, who responded with casual abandon, "Do not worry. I can manage."

Allonushea cooked the eggs and said, "Tomorrow morning I want you to go to the Czar and tell him that

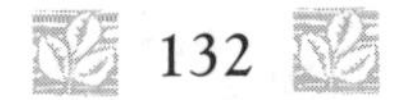

if he wants the chickens, he must find the one kind of grain for which you plow the field, sow the seed, harvest the grain, and collect the grain all in one day, and only then will my eggs be hatched, and that my chickens won't eat any other kind of grain." She added, "They will only eat this one kind of grain, which is called 'one-day grain.'"

So back to the Czar he went and told him what his daughter had said. The Czar said, "If your daughter is so wise, tell her to come and see me tomorrow, but she must not come on foot, nor on horse. And she must not bring any gifts, but she must not come without gifts. And she must not be naked, but she must not wear clothes."

The poor man walked back home thinking aloud, "My daughter won't be able to solve this problem. She might have had the answers to the previous riddles, but this one, I am certain, she will not be able to answer."

Once home, he told Allonushea the problem and she replied, "Okay, go to the nearest forest and get me a live rabbit and a live quail."

The next day Allonushea draped a net around her, sat on the little rabbit and held the quail in her hand and rode off to the Czar's court. When she reached the Czar, she got off her rabbit and, still holding the quail in her hands, walked toward him. Before the Czar could take the quail, it suddenly flew away.

Allonushea had brought a present, but she really hadn't brought it because she hadn't given it to him. She hadn't come by foot and she hadn't come by horse—she came by rabbit. And she wasn't wearing any clothing, she was wearing netting.

The Czar was so very pleased and said, "Okay, if you are so wise and your father is so poor, what do you feed yourself?"

Allonushea answered, "My father fishes, there is a dry bank behind our house. He fishes on the dry bank and cooks the fish he catches."

The Czar exclaimed, "Oh, you stupid girl, how can anyone catch fish on a dry bank?"

Allonushea replied, "You call me stupid? How can you call me stupid if you can even consider that a cart gave birth to a colt?" The Czar was very happy with her and took her and her poor father into his court. He waited for her to grow up and then he married her.

One of the largest countries in the world, Russia is home to diverse peoples and cultures drawn from Europe, the Middle East, and Asia. Russian art, architecture and literature—especially its children's stories—are world-famous. Russia's climate, however, is cold, and economic change has made life difficult for many millions of people. To help, CARE has been providing health care and emergency food relief to poor Russians as well as medical supplies and equipment to Russian hospitals.

SERBIA

In Search of the Most Wonderful Thing

by Igor Milosz

A very long time ago in a very faraway land, there lived a King who had an only child, his daughter, the Princess Anna Maria. Since the Princess had come of age to be married, she had a great number of suitors. Of all the many suitors who came before him, the King liked equally three particular Princes, Prince Boyan, Prince Marko, and Prince Alexei. As he could not decide which of the three should have his daughter's hand in marriage, he called them forth and said to them, "Go, all of you, and travel the world. Whoever brings home the most wonderful thing shall become the Princess's husband!"

The three Princes, very eager to win the King's favor, set out immediately on their journeys, each of them taking opposite routes in search of the most wonderful thing.

Much time passed. The Princes traveled to very faraway places. Finally, Prince Boyan found a magic carpet that could fly through the air and transport whoever sat on it.

Then Prince Marko found a marvelous and infinitely powerful telescope. When he looked through its lens, he could see everything in the world, distances unimaginable. He could see the wonderful palaces of China and the many-colored snails at the deep depths of the oceans.

The third suitor, Prince Alexei, found a magical ointment, which had the power to cure every disease there was, and even bring the dead back to life.

All these three Princes were very far away from each other. But when Prince Marko looked through the lens of his remarkable telescope, he saw his rival suitor, Prince

Boyan, walking with the magic carpet thrown over his shoulders. And so he ran to join Prince Boyan.

Together, the two Princes peered through the powerful telescope's lens and they saw Prince Alexei in a faraway land carrying the pot of magical ointment. With Prince Boyan's magic carpet, the two flew many many miles to join Prince Alexei.

Though all three Princes were rivals, they were still goodhearted men who had always been close friends. They spent their time telling one another of their travels and of their discoveries. Then Prince Marko exclaimed suddenly, "Let us look through my telescope and see what our beloved Princess Anna Maria is up to!" As he looked through the powerful lens he became dismayed. "The Princess is very ill. She seems to be lying in her bed and looks extremely weak, almost near death," he said with a very sad tone. All three Princes were thunderstruck with this news.

Then suddenly Prince Alexei exclaimed, "Wait, we can cure the Princess with my magical ointment. Quick, we must return to the Kingdom!" And immediately Prince Boyan unrolled his carpet and all three jumped on it. They flew back to the Princess with the greatest speed, outdistancing even the strongest birds.

When the Princes reached the Kingdom, they rushed to the palace. The King graciously received them and said

in a dispirited and sad voice, "I am afraid none of you will be able even to ask for the Princess's hand. She is lying in bed very ill and will most likely die!"

Prince Alexei came forward. "Do not worry, Your Majesty," he said. "We will be able to save the Princess. Here in this pot is a magical ointment which can cure all diseases."

The King, desperate for anything that would save his daughter, said to Prince Alexei, "You have my permission to see her. Quick, make haste and go to her!"

Prince Alexei and the other two suitors rushed to the Princess's bedchambers. He put ointment on her hands and then lifted her hands to her nose so she could smell the ointment as well. Within minutes, the Princess was revived. No longer was she weak and pale looking!

The King, who was overjoyed, immediately declared, "Prince Alexei, since it is your wonderful magical ointment that has saved my daughter's life, you then shall have her hand in marriage."

Prince Alexei was also overjoyed. However, no sooner had the King made his choice than the other Princes jumped in to dispute Alexei's reward. Young Prince Marko exclaimed, "If it were not for my telescope, we would have never discovered that the Princess was on her deathbed!" Then young Prince Boyan chimed in, "If it

were not for my magic carpet, we would never have made it back in time to save the Princess from dying!"

The King, hearing this dispute between the three young suitors, could come up with only one solution. "My young princes, from what I have heard, I cannot justly give any of you my daughter's hand in marriage. All of you, as great friends, have contributed equally to saving her life. I, therefore, ask you instead to do the most noble thing and give up the idea of marrying her."

The three young Princes agreed that the King's decision was, in the end, a just one. And so they left the Kingdom and traveled to faraway lands and lived there as hermits.

The King, meanwhile, married the young Princess Anna Maria off to another prince who came from a faraway land. After many years war broke out in the Kingdom. The King, deciding it was too dangerous for his daughter to remain, sent her away by ship to a faraway country.

During the trip, a great violent storm took hold of the seas. Everyone on board perished. The ship crashed into pieces as it hit a rocky coastline. Only the Princess was washed ashore and survived. She regained her strength and found her way into a forest. She lived for the next few years on wild berries and herbs, and never saw or met anyone.

One day Princess Anna Maria wandered a little too far from her home and became lost. She came upon a cave, and to her great astonishment, the cave had a small door. The Princess was curious, and knocked gently on the door. A deep voice emanated from the cave: "Who is there?" And suddenly the door flew open, and there appeared an old man with a long, long beard that flowed from his chin to the ground. His white hair was in total disarray and he looked completely disheveled.

The Princess was frightened not only because of the strange man's appearance but because this was the first time in years that she had met any human being at all! The hermit opened his mouth and asked, "Pray, who may you be, my daughter?"

The Princess replied, "Oh, dear sir, I have come from a faraway land...." And she sat down and recounted her story to the old hermit. Because the Princess had not talked to anybody for so many years, she was so excited that she went beyond telling the hermit the story of the shipwreck. She continued on, telling him the story of the three young princely suitors, and how they saved her life with their magical telescope, carpet, and ointment. "And because they were equally responsible for saving me, my father, the King, thought it was only just that none of them could in the end marry me." She finished with a sigh.

As she concluded her story the old hermit burst out with a huge smile and said, "Look more closely at me, my princess. Do you not remember who I am. I am one of those Princes who had sought your hand in marriage. Here is my telescope." And with these words, Prince Marko pulled a long brass instrument from the corner of his cave.

"My two friends and rivals, Prince Boyan and Prince Alexei, all came out here to live in this forest after that day when we saved your life." Taking his telescope, Prince Marko peered through its lens. "In fact, we can see their caves right now. It has been a very long time since I saw them both. As you can see, Princess, we live as lonely old hermits."

Prince Marko took Princess Anna Maria by the hand and led her to the other Princes. To all of them, she recounted her story and told them of her subsequent marriage and the shipwreck that followed. The three Princes were thrilled to be reunited with Princess Anna Maria.

As much as they enjoyed being together again with the Princess, the Princes knew that she must return home. They knew that her father, the King, must be desperate with worry.

Together, they made the most wonderful gifts they could for the Princess. They gave her the telescope, the magic carpet, and the ointment. They put the Princess on the magic carpet, and she flew back to her father.

The King was overjoyed to have his daughter back. Both he and the Princess would never forget the kind deed of these three friends and suitors. The Princes, who remained hermits all their lives, began to seek out each other's company, which had been spurred on by Princess Anna Maria's original visit. They spent many happy times telling each tales and lived happily ever after as the best of friends.

Serbia is a green and mountainous country in central Europe. Wracked by war and economic troubles in recent years, the Serbian people are in desperate need. CARE is providing emergency war relief such as food, medical supplies and support, clothing, school supplies and carpenter kits so that the Serbian people can start rebuilding their communities.

Latin American Stories

A Taste of Salt

Retold by Randi Becht
(Based on a Bolivian Folk Tale narrated in *Leyendas de mi tierra*)

In a small village located high in the Andes Mountains, there once lived the Indians Laracaja. During the famous War of the Warriors, which took place in Bolivia, these Native Americans fought for freedom from their rulers. Unfortunately, they lost the struggle and were forced to flee into the mountains.

There the survivors discovered a hidden place where they were completely protected by tall peaks and dense bushes. They built their homes with the firm intention of never again setting foot outside the mountains; only in this manner could they live in peace without being oppressed.

José Pacha was their proclaimed chief. He wrote and enforced the laws of the village. It was his intention to prevent his subjects from having any contact with people from the outside. He set guards to keep watch day and night. The guards saw to it that no one ever attempted to escape—for which the penalty was death.

Even with these restrictions, the people were happy. Don Pacha, as he was called, was a good leader and he provided the town with the most important goods needed for survival and comfort. He ordered that cotton be planted for fabric and clothes; corn, wheat, and potatoes were harvested for food. In this way, the people managed to live a simple, but comfortable life for many years.

One of the happiest families was that of Manuel Cito and his wife, Juana. Their only child was a daughter named Tiluca, who was thirteen years old and had an insatiable curiosity. Instead of playing with the other children, she hid behind rocks and bushes, listening to

what other people were saying. Mostly, she loved to eavesdrop on the elders, because they told stories of people who lived far away, outside their valley. Once she heard these stories, Tiluca wished more than anything else to visit these people and their unknown world.

One day, while listening to the elders, Tiluca overheard them speak of the wonderful taste salt adds to food. The girl, who, until now, had never heard of this peculiar spice, felt an incredible urge to taste salt for herself. So anxious was she to try it that an idea crept into her mind, and she secretly began to plan an escape from the village to find salt.

Determined that her plan should not fail, Tiluca set out to work diligently. She gathered tree branches and leaves until she had a large amount.

The next day, using the branches and leaves, she covered her entire body until she appeared to be nothing but a common bush on the ground. So disguised, she waited for nightfall.

As soon as darkness covered the little village, Tiluca crawled carefully along the ground until she approached the main gate. Unfortunately, a guard stood watch at the entrance. Tiluca waited a long time, hoping that some miracle would happen. Suddenly it came: the grunts of a hedgehog! Taking his lance, the guard sped after the wild pig and Tiluca seized this chance to escape.

Tiluca jumped over the rocks as fast as she could, then ran into the dense forest. Once there, she left her costume of leaves and began to make her way through the unknown land.

She walked for miles and miles, until she came upon a small town, which she cautiously entered by one of its many dusty streets. Not forgetting her mission, she began asking the people if they had any salt. One woman, who owned a small shop, told Tiluca that she had some and proceeded to show her.

Seeing the sparkling chunks of salt, Tiluca knew that her efforts had been worthwhile, and taking a piece in her hand, she asked the shopkeeper, "May I have this small amount?"

The woman replied, "I am sorry, little girl, I cannot give it to you. You see, I am very poor and do not make enough money."

Tiluca did not know what to do. She did not know what money was. Then she remembered that around her neck she was wearing a little gold pebble her father had given her. She offered this to the shopkeeper, who, with wide eyes, accepted her offer and gave Tiluca as much salt as she could carry.

It was still dark when Tiluca returned to her village. She covered herself with the same branches and leaves she had disguised herself in before and slipped past the gate

without being seen. Then, making sure that her parents had not noticed her absence, she went to hide her treasure in a small hole at the foot of her favorite tree.

Every night Tiluca broke off a small piece of salt for the next day. She hid it inside her pocket until mealtime and then sprinkled some on her food. Her parents soon noticed that Tiluca's appetite had increased. She even licked the last drop of her once-tasteless corn soup. This went on for several months until one day Tiluca noticed that she was about to take the last piece of precious salt.

Her last piece of salt now gone, Tiluca had to eat the again bland corn soup. It was with the hardest effort that she swallowed every spoonful. Finally, Tiluca stopped eating altogether and became very, very ill. Her worried parents sent for the medicine man, who was very surprised to hear the delirious Tiluca beg for salt. He realized at once what had happened and immediately told Don Pacha, who then ordered his guards to keep their eyes on Tiluca.

One night Tiluca dreamed that she escaped the village a second time in search of salt. She woke up immediately and felt as if her sickness were gone. It was still night and Tiluca silently got out of bed, dressed herself, and sneaked out through the streets toward the main gate.

The guards were asleep and she felt that once again her dream would come true. But as she reached the gate Tiluca felt a pain in her chest and let out a cry. All of a sudden the guards awoke and saw her. They grabbed the fugitive and took her to their chief.

Following the village laws, José Pacha would have had to condemn Tiluca to death for her crime. But seeing that she was only a disobedient young girl, he felt pity for her and sentenced her to prison for one year.

Tiluca was taken to a dark, damp cell. She felt very lonely, as no one was allowed to visit her, and her illness worsened until finally, weak and disheartened, Tiluca lay down on her pallet and died.

The guards took her body and buried it at the foot of her favorite tree, leaving no mark as to where she was buried, since no one was supposed to know of her attempted escape.

Tiluca's parents had not been told that she had been sentenced to prison and believed she had disappeared. They asked everyone in the village if they had seen Tiluca, but no one knew. Brokenhearted, they spent day and night crying at the foot of their daughter's favorite tree.

Then one day something strange occurred. The grass at the foot of the tree began to dry up, the earth became coarse, and a mysterious liquid emerged, which turned

into a white powder when it dried in the hot sun. The powder was pure salt!

It was never known whether the girl's bones decayed and, magically, turned into salt or whether her parents' constant tears supplied the salt. Maybe it was a little of both. But the truth is that from then on, the Laracaja Indians had their own fountain of salt to flavor their food.

Bolivia:

Bolivia is a lush, mountainous country in the center of Latin America. It was once the heart of the ancient Inca Empire. Bolivians today still wear the colorful patterns and clothes of their Indian ancestors. A poor country, Bolivia is assisted by CARE through lifesaving programs in health care, water and sanitation, and agriculture and environmental improvement, programs.

The Richest Coffee Bean

by Lauren Penchina Gomberg

Brazil is known to the world for its gift of rich coffee. A long time ago it was but a sole coffee bean that enabled a weary traveler to harvest the riches of an entire village. Some mistakenly believed coffee beans harbored magic powers. Evidence of the magic was the fact that those who regularly drank great quantities were more energetic and able to work longer before sleep set in, and animals that nibbled on growing coffee plants were more playful and alert.

It was fall, and the air was sweet with the scent of bright red berries, the fruit of the coffee tree. All were busy on the *fazenda* (plantation), stripping the berries off by hand onto canvas cloth spread under the trees. Others were loading baskets to be placed into streams of water that would carry the fruit to processing sheds. It was there that the pulp would be divided from the fruit, leaving the beans to dry in the air and the sun.

The entire countryside was absorbed in the gathering of the valuable crop, the strength of which would determine their fortune for the coming year. As they continued happily along in the process a beggarlike man appeared. He was gaunt and his clothes were tattered; still, he looked down into his hands with a big smile as though he had no worries at all. He walked up and down the *fazenda,* past the beans drying on the floor, past the area where beans were being bagged in burlap sacks, and past a number of workers stopping to break for a cool sip of water. All were curious as to why this scruffy man was gazing at his hands so happily.

"You there," yelled one of the coffee farmers. "What's that you have in your hands?"

The beggar turned his eyes toward the voice, and as his face lit up he said, "I have in my hand the most magnificent of beans...a special bean, an enchanted bean. I have traveled through many villages so they may prosper from the brew of this bean. This bean," he continued, "is the rarest of strains. It has the strength of thousands. It has a richness and a taste like none other in the world."

The people in the village began to listen intently. All were sharecroppers, with no chance of amassing great wealth. That is, unless they uncovered a new strain of coffee, a strain that would take half the time to harvest and command two, three, or even four times the price.

"Please, kind sir," asked a woman, "may we try your brew?"

"Yes, yes," others joined in, "let us try your enchanted brew."

"I'm afraid that can't be done," said the beggarlike man. "I am afraid this bean is not ready to be brewed. It must stay in the sun a few days longer in order for the strength of its full flavor to develop. It must be watched and turned and nurtured only by one who has worked with this kind before. I am so tired from my travels; I am not sure I have the energy or concentration needed to

nurture this bean. I will have to move on until I feel rested enough to give it the care it requires."

The villagers spoke quietly among themselves until a kindly gentleman stepped forward.

"Please, come and stay with me. I have a small home on the plantation, but you can get some rest while beginning to sun-dry the bean."

"I'm afraid I did not bring a change of clothes," answered the beggarlike man.

"Don't worry," answered a round-faced woman. "I have sewn clothes for much of my family, I will begin work on a new set of clothes for you tonight," she finished.

Starting that evening, the beggarlike owner of the bean was given a warm and comfortable place to stay. The following day his new set of clothes was completed. After the dawn of two days the villagers approached him, asking him if it was time to begin the brew.

"It is too dark tonight, I will begin the brew tomorrow," said the man, looking less like a beggar from two comfortable nights of sleep and his new set of clothes.

The next day he began to put the bean in a huge dark pot as the people gathered around.

"Hum." He sighed as he filled the kettle with water. "This can not be done. No one can create such a magical brew as this without the right ingredients. I'm afraid

I have chosen the wrong village." He began to turn away from the pot and wave good- bye.

"Wait," the townspeople stated. "What is it that we can do to help? We know we are not a wealthy village, but we have high hopes for your bean. What is it that you need to make your magical brew? Please don't leave; you have chosen the right town."

"Well," he said, "the bean must be surrounded by fruit."

And with that, the villagers scurried off, returning with figs, pineapples, custard apples, mangoes, bananas and guavas.

"I will have to use this a little at a time," he said. He packed some of the fruit into a large rumpled sack he was carrying and put a small amount in the kettle with the bean. Then, once again, a look of sadness crept upon his face.

"I'm afraid this fruit is not working. I will have to go elsewhere, perhaps where I can surround the bean with smoked and salted meats that will coax the magic out of the bean."

"Wait," the villagers responded. Before long they were back around the kettle with beef tongue, pig's tail, sausage, pig's feet and other village favorites.

Again the beggarlike man put some in the sack. "I must be careful as to how I proceed to make the brew, and I can see that something is not right. The people of the last plantation added rice, corn, potatoes, and soybeans to the kettle, yet we have none of these in our mixture."

The people hurried off, and once again they brought back what he had requested. Once again the man put some of the ingredients in his sack and added the others to the pot. But this time the man lit a fire under the pot and began to stir his concoction. Once again a look of dismay crept across his face. "There are too many birds in the sky. They are disturbing the natural harmony. We will need music to drown them out," said the man.

So, once again the townspeople obliged as a group of musicians began to play a rhythmic samba. As the music played the man went back to attend to the kettle. He stirred and he stirred until finally it was ready. As is the custom in Brazil, the no-longer beggarlike man served what he had made as part of the *almoco* (or middle-of-the-day luncheon).

The villagers were quite impressed. It was the most delicious thing they had ever eaten. Still, they were anxious to unleash the magic of the bean and to travel the road to wealth and riches through the harvest of an entire crop of such beans. At the close of the meal, the man reached into the pot and handed a lead farmer the sole bean.

"Here," he said, "here is the magic bean." With that he took his sack and was on his way.

Once they had waved good-bye, the villagers planted the sole bean as they had been instructed by the man, and began to wait for the magical crop.

But months later all they discovered was a sole coffee plant with red fruit like any other coffee plant they had ever planted. By now the man had been long gone. They realized they had been foolish and simple to believe in a magic brew, yet they were not sorry. Although the preparation of the brew had not brought them wealth or magic, it had been a welcome break from the demands of the coffee harvest. The village decided that every year, during the harvest, they would take an afternoon out for a similar celebration.

BRAZIL:

The largest country in Latin America, and one of the largest countries in the world, Brazil has an enormous diversity of plants, animals and people (including Portuguese, Africans, Italians, Germans, Japanese, Indians, Jews and Arabs). CARE packages went to refugees from World War II who settled there. Brazil is also home to the endangered Amazon rain forest, which covers approximately half of the entire country. One of the world's largest forest and river areas, the Amazon has in recent years become increasingly threatened by the logging, farming and mining industries.

Middle Eastern Stories

EGYPT

The Royal Candlestick

Retold by Hasan M. El-Shamy,
Professor of Folklore
at Indiana University

Once there was a merchant who had a single son. Every day he gave him fifty pounds or twenty-five pounds and said to him, "Spend, son! When you are finished, come back to me for more."

One day the boy said to himself, "Is my father making this money or what? Every day he gives me twenty-five or fifty pounds to spend."

He went to his father and said, "Father, I want a hundred pounds to go away and start a trade."

His father said, "Son, there's nothing that you are missing. You are getting everything. Why do you want to go away?"

The son answered, "Impossible; I must go and start a trade."

The father gave him a hundred pounds, and the boy's mother also gave him her necklace and said, "Any time you need more money, take it out of this necklace."

Now the boy took the hundred pounds and spent it in one day. He spent it immediately, not on sinful things but on the poor. He had nothing left with him except the necklace. He said to himself, "Now that I have wasted all the hundred pounds without starting a trade or anything, what am I going to go back and tell my father? The best thing is to run away."

He readied himself and walked along the bank of the river. He walked and walked and walked. Finally he met a fisherman. He said to the fisherman, "Fisherman, cast your net once for me to see my luck."

The fisherman cast his net and pulled. There was nothing in it except a small brass box.

"Give it to me."

"By God, I will not give it to you except for a hundred pounds!"

"A hundred pounds for this box!"

"Yes, a hundred pounds."

"I have nothing except a necklace. This necklace."

The fisherman said to him, "All right, give it to me."

The boy handed the hundred-pound necklace over to him, took the box, and now had nothing at all with him. He took the box and walked away.

He walked and walked and walked until he came to a deserted place. The boy was very hungry. He said to himself, "Already you have wasted your two hundred pounds, and now you haven't even got the price of a meal. What are you going to do?"

He thought, Why don't I open this box and see what's in it?

He opened the box, and inside he found an exact replica of a human being, whose size was the exact size of the box. The moment he opened the box, the thing said to him, "I am at your command."

"'At your command'! What's this?"

It answered him, "I came out to you because of your luck. Ask for anything and you'll get it."

The boy said to it, "I'm hungry."

It answered, "Close your eyes and then open them."

He closed his eyes, and when he opened them, he

found a table with every good thing on it. He sat down and ate. When he was finished, he folded his table, put away the things, took his box, and went on.

He walked and walked and walked until he came to a different country. On the border of this country he came to a town. At the edge of this town there was a palace. From the foundation up, this palace was built of human skulls.

"What's this?"

Every time he asked somebody, "Why is this palace this way?" no one would answer him.

Finally he went to a tobacco seller. The tobacco seller said to him, "I have Cotarelli, Belmonts, and this and that."

The boy asked him, "Tell me, why is this palace the way it is?"

The tobacco seller answered him, "Ask this old woman."

He asked the old woman who was sitting nearby. He said to her, "Maternal aunt, tell me, why is this palace the way it is?"

She answered him, "By God, son, our king has a daughter who does not speak. The King has offered his daughter to the young men of the country. He gave them the condition that he who stays with her for three days and makes her talk will marry her at the

end of these three days. But he who fails will have his head cut off."

"All these people died because of that?"

"Yes," she answered him.

He went to a corner, took his box out, opened it, and said to our friend inside it, "This is your day. They say that the King's daughter does not speak. Will you be able to make her speak?"

The little man said to him, "Yes! When you get inside, put me underneath the candlestick" (for in the old days they did not have electricity; they had only candles).

Now where did the boy go? He went to the King. The boy said to the King. "I'm asking for your daughter."

The King said, "Son, you are too young. It is a shame that you should die; traces of good living still show on you. Why don't you go away? Look at all these heads."

The boy answered him, "I am just like those to whom they belonged."

"Is that so?"

"Yes, that is so."

"All right, get the witnesses. Get the judge. Write."

The boy wrote, signed, and said, "Put your seal on it."

The King put his seal on it and said, "Take him to her."

They took him to the room of our lady. Before she entered, he put his box underneath the candlestick.

He said to her, "My lady, daughter of kings."

She did not utter a word.

"Peace be upon you. How do you do? Queen. You who are this. You who are that."

She was just like a piece of stone sitting on a chair.

He said to her, "All right, if a human being cannot keep me company, then maybe the candlestick will."

He turned to the candlestick and said, "Peace be upon you, royal candlestick."

The candlestick replied—that other one from beneath the candlestick replied, "And upon you be God's peace and his mercy, son of kings."

The boy said to him, "Why don't you tell us a story instead of this sad time we are having?"

He answered him, "All right, I'm going to tell you a story."

"What's the story, candlestick?"

"Once there were three brothers. They had one *bint 'Aam* (paternal uncle's daughter). This one said, 'I'll marry her!' And that one said, 'No! I'll marry her! The third one said, 'No! I'll marry her.'

"People in their country decided, 'All three of you will take a trip. He who brings back the most precious things will marry her.'

"So the three got their things and left. Finally, the road branched out into three different roads: the road of safety, the road of sorrow, and the road of no return. Each one of the brothers went down one of these roads.

"The one who went down the road of no return finally came to the spring of the water of life. He took some.

"The one who went down the road of safety found a carpet which when struck would fly.

"The third one found a mirror. This mirror could show him anything in the whole universe.

"Finally, all of them met on the same road. The one with the mirror said to them, 'Brothers, our cousin is dying.'

The one with the carpet said, 'Let's go!'

Immediately they were there. The girl was almost dead. They were dripping water into her mouth drop...by...drop. The brother with the water of life gave her some, and immediately she got up, as if she had never been sick."

Now all of this was told by the candlestick to the boy. The candlestick asked the boy, "Who should marry the girl? If it weren't for the mirror, they wouldn't have seen her. If it weren't for the carpet, they wouldn't have reached her in time. If it weren't for the water of life, she wouldn't have been revived. Now who should marry her?"

The boy answered, "Of course, the one with the water of life."

Now the one who was completely dumb spoke eloquently. She said, "Glory be to God, how strange-natured we are! If it weren't for the one with the mirror, they wouldn't have seen her dying, they wouldn't have reached her, and they wouldn't have revived her. She should go to the one with the mirror."

The moment the girl spoke, the boy pulled the loose sofa cover over his head and said, "Ekkk! You have a bad mouth odor!"

The judges who were watching them were surprised. The King's daughter, who hadn't spoken a word all her life, was now talking like a rattler! No, that couldn't be! They had better wait until tomorrow.

The judges left, and the boy pretended to be asleep. Now the girl started talking to the candlestick. Wanting what? Wanting the candlestick to converse with her as it had with the boy.

"Peace be upon you, royal candlestick!...Peace be upon you, royal candlestick!"

Nothing. The girl was furious, and hit, hit, hit, until she broke the candlestick.

In the morning our friend took his box out from beneath the broken candlestick. He said to it, "Now where am I going to put you?"

The box answered, "Put me underneath the chair."

He put it underneath the chair.

At night the girl entered the room again. The boy started talking to her. The more the boy talked, the more the girl remained silent. The boy finally said, "All right, since the human cannot keep us company, maybe the chair will. Peace be upon you, royal chair."

"And upon you be peace, king's son."

"Tell us a story to keep us company, royal chair."

The chair said, "All right, I will. Once, three persons were traveling together—a carpenter, a tailor, and a sheikh, an *'ustaz* (a religious savant, I mean). Finally they came to a lonely area. By night they divided themselves into three shifts. Two would sleep, and the third would stay on guard.

"The first third of the night, who was awake? The carpenter. While the sheikh and tailor were asleep, the carpenter found a piece of wood. He made a doll out of it.

"At midnight he went to sleep, and the tailor took over. The tailor found the doll; it was almost human, but it was naked. He took out his sewing machine, and tick, tick, tick, tick, tick—he made her a dress.

"At the end of the night our friend the worshiper saw the girl before his eyes, almost perfect and dressed, but with no soul. He prayed to God to give a soul to this girl. God accepted his prayer, and the doll became a human being.

"Each one of the three said, 'She is mine!'

"Now, son of kings, who should marry the girl?" (That's what the chair was asking the boy.)

The boy answered, "The *'ustaz,* naturally."

The girl said, "Praise be to God, how strange you are. Had it not been for the carpenter who made the doll in the first place, there would have been no girl. The carpenter should marry her!"

The boy turned his face away and said, "Ekkkk! Your mouth has a bad odor."

Now the judges who were standing by went to the King.

"King, now for two nights your daughter has spoken."

"My daughter?"

"Yes."

"Well, let's see what's going to happen on the third night."

Now, after the girl had spoken, the boy pretended to be asleep. The girl spoke to the chair. "Royal chair."

The chair did not answer.

"Honored chair."

The chair did not answer.

"Our property..."

The girl became furious and broke the chair into pieces.

In the morning the boy took his box out and asked it, "Now where am I going to hide you?"

The box said, "Hide me underneath your turban. She can't do a thing to it."

That night when the girl came, the boy spoke to her, but still she did not answer. "Our dear daughter. Our dear friend. You have spoken for two nights; speak now."

She didn't utter a word. The boy said, "All right, the first night she broke the candlestick. The second night she broke the chair. These were her property. Now my very own turban, peace be upon you."

The turban replied, "And upon you be God's peace and mercy, master. What do you want?"

The boy said, "Tonight why don't you put on a show? We want stage shows and dances."

From underneath the turban came seven girls. This one was playing the castanets, this one the drum, that one dancing. All of them were wonderful, gi-n-a-a-a-n (cr-a-a-azy)!

The boy watched all night. Finally the girl, the King's daughter, threw herself at the boy. The boy pushed her away and said, "Go away. Don't you see I have got all those who are better than you are?"

She became jealous; these girls were very beautiful.

The judges went to the King and said, "King. Now for three days your daughter has been speaking. And now she is just dying over the boy. She is throwing herself on him."

The King wondered, “My own daughter? Spoke three nights! And now is throwing herself on the boy! I have to see this with my own eyes.”

“Come along.”

The King went to find his daughter naked. When he saw her, he screamed in amazement. “What are you doing, daughter! What’s this?”

She answered him, “The whole world is like this. I hadn’t seen the world, nor have I entered it yet.”

The King ordered celebrations to be made. They gave wedding parties and beautiful celebrations. The King married his daughter to this boy. The boy took over the Kingdom, and they lived in stability and prosperity.

The towering Pyramids of Giza and the monumental stone Sphinx come to mind when one thinks of this ancient country and culture. Egyptian history dates back to 4000 B.C., and its archaeological ruins, art, literature, and philosophy influenced the entire world. Today, its hot, dry climate and growing population has created increased poverty. CARE helps poor Egyptians by teaching farmers to grow more and better food, by offering health services to families and by building water and sanitation systems for struggling communities.

Boastfulness Versus True Generosity

by Blanche L. Serwer-Bernstein

Once there was a great and famous Caliph of Baghdad, Haroun al-Rashid, who was well-liked by his people, but had one great fault known to all: he boasted that no man alive gave as splendid gifts as he did. His pride and arrogance came between him and his people.

This worried his chief minister, the Grand Wazir Jafar, whose reputation for loyalty to the Caliph provided him with the courage to broach the subject with the ruler.

After kissing the ground three times at the Caliph's feet, Jafar said, "O Commander of the Faithful, forgive your humble servant Jafar for daring to remind you that a true believer is always humble before Allah. He never boasts of his riches or his generosity. It would be nobler of you, O Caliph, to leave it to your subjects to praise you for your generous gifts."

The Caliph's face became red and his eyes flashed his fury. "Miserable Wazir," he roared, "don't you know that to tell me a lie is a crime punishable by death?"

"I speak the truth," answered Jafar, prostrating himself before the Caliph. "When I was last in Basra, I was the guest of this fine young man, Abu Ahmad, and I was astonished at his generosity and his humility. He must have endless treasures of a most unusual quality, for his gifts are unique, and he gives them freely. If you do not believe me, O Caliph, send a message to Basra to test my words."

The Caliph was so furious that he could not speak. He signaled to his guards, who grabbed hold of Jafar and dragged him off to prison.

The Caliph stalked out of the room and went straight to the apartment of his queen, Zobeide, where he flung himself down on a sofa without uttering a word.

The Queen was upset when she saw how angry he was, but she was too wise to ask him what was wrong. She poured him a glass of rose-scented water and murmured, "The blessings of Allah be with you. Some days are filled with gloom and some with joy. May all your days be filled with happiness, my lord."

Her sweet voice had a calming effect on him, as always. He drank the rose water slowly. In a relaxed mood, he told her all about his altercation with his Wazir.

The clever Queen understood that Jafar's life was in danger. She did not think it wise to defend him at that moment to her irate husband. She did agree, however, that a messenger to Basra might easily discover the truth about the young man's generosity.

"That is only just," admitted the Caliph, "and I do want to be fair. Jafar has always been faithful to me and loyal to our country. I will not have him hanged until I am certain about the truthfulness of his report. But since there is no one else I can trust, I will dress in disguise and go to Basra myself."

That very day the Caliph set out alone by camel from Baghdad to Basra, dressed as a traveling merchant. Allah took him safely to Basra, where he went directly to the best inn in the city.

The Caliph immediately inquired of the innkeeper, "Is it true that there is in Basra a young man named Abu Ahmad, known for his wealth and his generosity, who gives more splendid gifts than any king?"

"Indeed there is," replied the innkeeper. "The blessings of Allah be on him! If I had a hundred mouths and the same number of tongues in each mouth, I would not be able to give his generosity the full praise it deserves."

The Caliph was still incredulous. After seeing to the care of his camel, he had his supper and retired for the night.

After breakfast the next morning he set out on foot. On the way he stopped off to ask a shopkeeper in the bazaar the way to Abu Ahmad's house.

"If you do not know that"—the shopkeeper said smiling—"you must have come from far away. Abu Ahmad is better known in Basra than any king in his capital city. I will send my son to guide you."

When the Caliph reached Abu Ahmad's home, he saw a splendid palace, built of light pink marble with great doors of green jade. He said to the doorkeeper, "Go tell your master that a stranger has come from Baghdad especially to visit him."

Abu Ahmad immediately descended to the courtyard to welcome his unexpected visitor. After they had greeted each other in the name of Allah, Abu Ahmad led his guest into a hall of remarkable beauty. They seated themselves on a soft couch of green silk embroidered with gold, which extended around the four sides of the hall.

Abu Ahmad clapped his hands and twelve male attendants entered, carrying cups of agate and rock crystal, set with rubies and filled with the finest red wine. They were followed by twelve female attendants, beautiful as the full moon in a cloudless sky, bearing porcelain basins of fruit and flowers and large golden goblets of sherbet covered with cream as white as snow. The Caliph had never tasted anything so delicious, although the finest food and drink in the Eastern world were brought to his palace daily.

Abu Ahmad then led him to a second hall, more splendid than the first. There, delicious fish and chicken and meats were served on golden dishes.

Finally, they went into a third chamber for desserts. Light pastries, jam, and honey were served, followed by white and red wines in golden goblets.

As they ate, sweet singers and gifted instrumentalists entertained them. The Caliph was especially moved by the tone of the lute music, and praised the sound to Abu Ahmad.

The Caliph never expected such a meal and such a concert on earth. It all seemed to be taking place in Heaven.

Abu Ahmad excused himself politely and left the hall for a moment. When he returned, he was carrying an amber wand in one hand and in the other a little tree of silver adorned with leaves of emeralds and fruits of rubies.

He set the tree in front of the Caliph, who saw that there was a golden peacock of rare workmanship perched on the top of it. Abu Ahmad touched the bird with his amber wand. It immediately stretched its golden wings and spread the jeweled splendor of its tail. Then it began to rotate quickly, sending out little jets of perfume that filled the hall with a heavenly scent. No sooner had the Caliph shown an interest and settled down to watch this wonder than Abu Ahmad carried it off.

This is strange behavior, thought the Caliph angrily, snatching it away before I have my fill of watching the bird. It doesn't appear as if Abu Ahmad understands how to be generous!

Abu Ahmad came back carrying a cup carved from a single giant ruby and filled with purple wine. He gave it to the Caliph, who drank all the wine, the finest he had ever tasted. To his surprise, the cup filled itself with wine at once. He emptied it again, and once more it filled itself.

He could not refrain from asking his host, "How does this miracle happen?"

"The cup was made by a wise and holy man who knew all the secrets of nature," replied Abu Ahmad, taking the cup from the Caliph and hurrying out of the hall.

By my life, thought the Caliph, his anger increasing, "this young man has no idea of good manners. As soon as he sees I am pleased with anything, he snatches it away. When I return to Baghdad, I will teach my Wazir Jafar to be a better judge of men and to turn his tongue around his mouth before he speaks. I had better leave before I lose my temper!"

When his host returned, the Caliph arose and said, "Abu Ahmad, I am overcome by the generosity you have shown me, an unknown stranger. Allow me to leave you to your rest, for I must not trespass further on your kindness."

The young man bowed, not wishing to detain his guest beyond his desire to remain. He accompanied the Caliph to the palace gate, where he said, "I beg you to forgive me for having given you entertainment unworthy of so delightful a visitor." They bowed to each other and parted.

The Caliph walked back to the inn muttering furiously to himself, "That young fool did nothing but show off his riches and treasures to me. Generous, indeed! I'll teach Jafar what happens to anyone who lies to me!"

He was still fuming when he reached the inn. At the gate he found a line of Abu Ahmad's attendants, each carrying on a brocaded cushion one of the desirable objects that had been displayed in the palace.

A young attendant handed the Caliph a scroll of silk paper. He unrolled it and read these words: "The peace of Allah be upon a charming guest, whose coming brought happiness! It seemed to me that you were not displeased by these objects, which I now put before you: the lute whose music you seemed to enjoy, the wine cup, and the tree. I hope you will accept them from one whose house you have honored. Abu Ahmad."

"By the honor of my ancestors!" cried the Caliph. "How I have misunderstood this young man! Where is my generosity now? It is nothing compared with his! O faithful Jafar, how right you were to rebuke me for my pride and boasting!"

He called for pen and ink and fine silk paper and wrote a note in which he described his gratitude to Abu Ahmad. He gave it to the smallest of the attendants to deliver to his master. Then he returned with Abu Ahmad's gifts to the palace in Baghdad.

His first official act upon his return was to release Jafar from his dungeon and give him a robe of honor to show the whole court that he was reinstated as the grand wizar. Then he told Jafar the story of his adventures and asked, "What can I do to reward this generous young man?"

"O Commander of the Faithful," answered Jafar, "you have confirmed that Abu Ahmad lives and behaves like a king, and is much beloved in his city. May I suggest that you make him King of Basra?"

"You are wise, Jafar," responded the Caliph. "Let the patent of royalty be drawn up for me to sign. Then, Wazir, you yourself will travel to Basra and bring Abu Ahmad here. He will be crowned in my presence so that we may rejoice together."

All this was done.

The great Caliph no longer boasted about the splendor of his gifts to others. Moreover, he spread throughout the caliphate the tale of Abu Ahmad's generosity.

Ancient Iraq's Tigris-Euphrates valley has been called the "Cradle of Civilization," for it was here that civilization began, according to legend. Iraq's capital city, Baghdad, later became the inspirational setting for many of the wonderful stories found in *The Arabian Nights.* Today Iraq is struggling to recover from the Persian Gulf

IRAQ

War. CARE is helping refugees at the border with Turkey, providing food, water, tents and blankets to 240,000 people a day.

An Invitation

An Invitation To Aspiring Folklore Storytellers

The stories in this book come from many different countries around the world. These stories are not only fun to read but also provide insight into that particular culture's traditions, customs and beliefs.

Folktales are part of an oral tradition. You do not have to be a professional writer to tell or write folktales. In fact, many of the stories you read in this book have mostly been told or retold by people (from college professors to farmers) who had heard the story from their grandparents or from friends who had the story passed along to them by someone else.

Because we know that all of our friends around the world had a lot of fun telling us their folktales for this book, we think American children who are descended from many different cultures can do the same for the next CARE folklore book.

We invite all children to submit stories. You can become a folktale writer by retelling stories that reflect your own cultural and regional backgrounds—stories that you have heard from your friends or families. Some stories will be selected for future publication in a new CARE folklore book that will feature stories written by children.

Use the stories in this book as a guideline—the stories should be long enough to tell the story well, but need not be longer than two or three pages. Please do not send us the original copy of your story, as we will be unable to send back material. But remember to include your name, address and phone number so that we may get in touch with you if your story is selected.

Please send stories to: Brian Sockin and Eileen Wong
c/o Co-Options, Inc.
66 Glenbrook Rd.
Ste. 4215
Stamford, CT 06902